The Art of Self-Destruction

Bigger on the Inside

By

4 A.M.

First Edition 2015

Published by Insomniatic Productions
Edited By Daryl Webster

A long winded Dedication/Foreword follows.

Being as this is the first of hopefully many Bundles of words to come, I couldn't Bring myself to place a standard dedication Here. So although long winded, I did this instead. Typing it out just felt too cheap.

This story, this entire series actually, is based off a short story I wrote back in the early 2000's, during a Thanksgiving spent in Hectorville Oklahoma

It was a battle to finish. But Now that it is complete, with a second nearly wrapped, and two more mapped out, and eager to be told, I feel that it is clearer to me now than ever before in the years passed.

Once I was able to string all the Right words together, the way they were meant to be, this world I'd created was so much easier to understand.

And without the presence, words, help, or motivation from these next few people, I never would have made it to this point.

To my Beautiful and Wonderful Wife.
Who would let me Rant and Rave
to her as I hit one mental hurdle After
another. Not so much helping me create
this story, But keeping me sane through
it. Which in hindsight, was A pretty
fucking important task. for forcing me
to sleep when I'd been up for days and
Became slightly delusional. for making me
Eat and drink something other than coffee,
Whiskey and cigarettes. for patiently trying
to calm me when I swore everything was
going wrong, talking to me like I wasn't
a complete madman. for putting up with
my "Episodes" when ignoring your advice
and dragging myself too far, for too long.
And for not breaking my face everytime
I lost my shit and acted like A complete
Ass.

I love you dear. I know I don't
say it enough, And probably Never Will.
But I do.

And Then There's Ronnie Midnight.
A Strange fellow, Which is Just the
Way I like 'EM.

My ideas and thoughts were Just adrift
in clouds of smoke, With no home or direction
Until I met you. You motivated me to
do more, To keep doing it Better Because
I had more in me. And then you gave
me the Tools to do it. Helped me to understand
the business, To understand the Reader, And
That I could do it, and still be bat shit crazy!
You are a Kind man, and through all our
delays, and our VERY Rough year of personal
lives, you always came into our conversations
Enthusiastic and optimistic. Which is Exactly
What I needed when I struggled along
Through this.

I'm glad to have met you my friend,
and I hope we have more years
of working Together ahead of us.

And finally, To Daryl Webster.
For working with me through all the
last minute changes, alterations, my
indecisive decision making, and some
really jumbled and crumpled late night/
early morning drafts that I was cranking
out. Your critiques, comments, positive
remarks, and real life comparisons helped
make this disaster so much better than
it would have BEEN.

I don't think I know a more respectable
man, and I'm thankful of the time you
took from your busy work and family
life to add some of your wise
insights to my story.

I'm sure there are many more
that I should be mentioning, but haven't.
Shoot me an email, I'll get ya on the
next book!
x

4 K.M.

And so we begin...

Sudden HeartBreak

Chapter One

The ringing wakes me. Sunshine piercing my
eyeballs like a syringe, the shrill noise
intensifying the pain. I hear a thousand starving
infants screaming in my head at once. I just want
to go back to sleep for another hour, maybe two,
maybe a full day. Anything to relieve this whore
of a hangover.

The mattress creaks loudly as I roll over,
groping for my phone, blindly, desperately, like my
solace lay within. My shaking hand comes back to me
empty. A groan escaping my mouth, but the noise
isn't my own, I'm almost positive. Something tight
is on my head, feeling for the foreign object, I
discover my shades. I slip them down over my eyes
like a shield from the evil forces raping my body
in the present. Sitting up from the bed, I forget

about the ringing phone for the moment. Off the corner of the writing desk beside the bed, I spot a half cigarette leaning on the ridge of a glass ashtray. I pop it in my mouth and lite it with the zippo from my very soggy jeans that I am still wearing.

Taking in the room around me, I cling to wisps of smoke quickly dissipating along with the memories of the night before. Across the room, the fish aquarium is pitch black, a siphon hose hanging over the edges, half the water missing. I rise to get a better look, and find the three fish inhabitants dead and bloated, "What the fuck?" I mumble out loud to no one but myself. On the ground to my left are the blinds that normally block this sunlight from peering into my room. They lie in a tattered heap, the bracket that holds them up snapped in half, and a broken bottle of beer fermenting on top of the whole mess. Thinking back, I vaguely recollect climbing in through the window last night, and I wasn't alone.

I remember the phone suddenly, I go back to the bed and pull away the lone sheet and pillow upon it. Nothing. I tug the mattress a few inches from the wall, "Found ya', bitch." Picking it up, the screen automatically illuminates with thirteen missed calls. Skimming through the calls, all of them are from Celia. *Well, this can't be good.* I hit the call button and wait as the phone begins ringing.

"Hello?" A voice too peppy for my liking answers.

"It's me. You okay?"

"Yeah. I am now. Are you?"

"I'm fine, why do you ask?"

"Oh, you know, the whole part where I waited at your apartment all night where we were supposed to talk last night?"

She's angry, I was pretty sure (insert sarcasm please, if you haven't already), "Didn't I call to tell you I was at Efren's last night?"

"Yeah, about two this morning after you didn't reply to any of my calls or text."

"I'm sorry. I must have gotten a bit carried away."

"Yeah. I'm at the CJ's down the street. Meet me."

Something to drink other than alcohol sounded delicious. My mouth tasted like I'd been licking a cat's asshole all night after a bad case of the runs. "I'll be there in about fifteen."

"Whatever." She hung up. Definitely mad. I stand debating in my mind whether or not I should change, then decide against it. A quick rinse sounds like a better idea, more to wash the stench of booze off than anything. Leaving the bedroom, I nearly trip over a guy passed out, laying on the floor of the hallway. Left and right I look, another five or six bodies lay there as well. Passed out drunk, or too high, they were the unfortunate few that didn't get to a couch or spare bedroom in time. I laugh a little.

Stepping over the first body, I hop over the next, I reach the bathroom with little delay. As I shut the bathroom door behind me, my bladder sends a signal to my brain, *game on man*. At times like these, the slider on my jeans always seems to go ape shit, it's flipped at a weird angle and you can't get hold of it. Or it's jammed with a flap of material or something stupid like that. Only when it's like, "If I don't go now, this shit is gonna be blasting."

Anyways, I feel the seconds ticking by while I fight my pants, finally escaping their stranglehold on me, and I'm instantly unloading a gallon or two of fuck me up from the night before. Dropping the cigarette into the toilet as I flush, I strip my jeans off, tear away my t-shirt, and step into the shower, spinning the knob full blast hot. I hold a hand under the nozzle while waiting for the warmth, then flip it up to the shower head. I'm dumping shampoo and soap on myself like it's going out of style, trying to get done with this as quickly as possible.

The bathroom door opens and shuts, I ignore it, I've got things to do. Then I hear someone peeing, a flush, I wait for the temperature change, but it isn't as drastic as I expected. The shower curtain is pulled away and in steps this naked girl I had never met before. "Uhh, hello there."

"Hi." She says, like this is no big deal. Which it is, because, you know, she's hot, and I'm pretty much living one of those dream porn scenes that all us animals with a penis have. She's thin, but not anorexic like, dark hair, tan all over, I'm staring down at her small, perky tits, she smiles before gently pushing me out from under the warmth of the water. "Don't remember me, do you?"

"If we've met before, please forgive me, I don't know how the sight of you would ever slip my memory."

"Smooth talker, even when you aren't shitfaced? Cute." She's lathering up with the soap, and my soldiers standing to salute. Then, boom, oh fuck, Celia. I'm trying to worm my way back in to get rinsed, "I'm Zoe. We met last night."

"I'm honestly, extremely hazy on last night at the moment. However, I'm sure, much to my chagrin, I will soon remember once this hangover subsides."

"Aww, you weren't bad. I hope you do remember though. It was the most fun I've had in a long while."

"In that case, I am pretty fuckin cool. Anyways, I gotta go."

"To see Celia?"

"How'd you know?"

"She called Efren last night when she couldn't find you. He made you call. It was pretty funny watching you try to sound sober."

"Oh boy, then I suspect this meeting I'm having with her will be short. I really gotta go though."

"I'll see ya when you get back."

"Uhh, okay then." I'm exiting the shower as fast as I can, trying not to slip on the tile, drying off hastily, drop the towel to the floor, pulling on the jeans, then the shirt, escaping the bathroom, finally. Swiping a pack of smokes from my jacket that hung near the entry door, and my hat, I step out into the hot morning. My shoes are on the porch, still wet from the night before. That part, I do remember. I lite another smoke and start walking towards the CJ's at the end of the block barefoot.

Fresno, California is a fucked up town. I've lived all over this god awful place. People always tell me, live in any city long enough and you're bound to see the dirt. I strongly disagree. Living in several different cities through my life, this place was like a shart on a long walk home. But hey, to each their own.

Trying to make quick steps through Efren's neighborhood, I come up to First Street, then continue north. As I approach the daycare center on my left, I hear screams and laughter from children. Huddled at the side of the building, a couple of the adults smoke cigarettes, probably bitching about the little bastards they watch all day. I laugh to myself, a little too loudly, I realize as the group looks over at me irritated. Continuing down the sidewalk, I notice the bagel joint has a line out the door, and wonder how bad you really must want a bagel to wait in that line. Then, with sudden heartbreak, I see a going out of business sign hanging on the window of the small bookstore beside it. I shake my head, wondering how people can let something like that happen when there's a (*INSERT MAJOR COFFEE CHAIN HERE*) on every corner of the block.

In the parking lot of Cj's I spot Celia's car. Cutting through the lot, hurrying towards the entrance of the restaurant, I see her through the window drinking something from a coffee cup. Tea, she never drank coffee.

The cool air blows against my body as I open the door, it feels good, hadn't realized I was already sweating.

"For one?" the hostess asks as I walk by.

"Meeting someone." I walk past her without a glance, in a rush to see what kind of pissed off Celia is. I slide my ass into the booth across from her. We never sit together anymore, not since maybe the third or fourth date. Is that weird? She doesn't even look at me, just stares down at her tea, which I can smell from where I sit. Something bitter, with a sweetness that reminded me of Tang.

"How are you?" I ask, watching closely for some reaction to give me an inkling about how this conversation is about to go. As she looks up at me, I can tell immediately she's been crying. Her eyes are bloodshot and puffy. "Are you okay?" I try to sound concerned, but my words come out flat instead. Always been that way, never good with emotion, other than lust and anger.

"I'm pregnant." The words leave her throat, and mine tightens with a knot. "It isn't yours." Well fuck me. "I loved you so much. But you kept pushing me further and further away. You're broken, I know you had some bad shit happen, but it's time to get over it already. I know you won't though, you just find fix after fix. I don't even know how you find enough focus to write anymore. It really does amaze me. Your mind, it's so brilliant. You write and draw these beautiful stories and scenes. How something so perfect comes out of a mind as fucked up as yours, I've got no idea."

And at this point, yeah, I still say nothing.

"I grabbed my things from the apartment already. I hope you find something or someone that makes you want to live again. All you are right now is a withering shell of a man that is lost in a trance, going about the motions to make sure he stays that way. Frankly, it's pretty sad and pathetic." With that, she rises, places a ten on the table, and walks out.

The waitress glides over to my table with a smirk, eavesdropping the whole time. "All done here?" She makes a grab for the ten, I quickly snatch it before she can.

"She just had the tea?"

"Yes." She looks confused, and a little annoyed.

"Let me get a coffee then, same check. How much would the total on that be?"

Angrily she scribbled with her pen on the notepad she had in hand, "$9.97."

"Good." I give her the ten, "Keep the rest, you earned it." I say with a smile. So what if she spits in my coffee. Coffee's fucking coffee when you're this hungover and having this kind of day.

I slug down the coffee too quick. It burns like a bitch. I just need the caffeine and I'll start to feel better. I've done the drill enough to know my body's needs. The last drop hits my tongue and I start to walk out, flipping the waitress the bird as I pass her again.

The heat seems to have doubled since I've been inside. Sweat beads made of liquor spawn upon my brow instantly. "Fuck this." I walk fast, trying to get home as quick as possible, I feel the vomit coming, the batch of evil gone worse boiling in my stomach. I make it all the way to the porch before I realize I can't hold it. Leaning over the steps, I unswallow into the rose garden. I continue to retch twice more; I hear the door open. Efren is standing in nothing but a pair of boxers, he hands me a jug of apple juice, my hangover pick me up. I chug a few mouthfuls, then another to swish around my mouth and spit out with the vomit. We retreat from the heat into the house. He shuts the door, then leads me into the dining room.

I take the closest seat at the round, wooden table surrounded by four, wooden chairs. Efren walks over to the coffee pot and pours two glasses as I drink some more apple juice. He sets a cup in front of me, "For when you're ready."

"Thanks." I take another swig, then put the cap on the juice, pushing it to the side of the table, then start sipping at my coffee.

"Went that bad?" he asks while lighting a cigarette and picking up the morning paper.

"She's pregnant."

He dipped the side of the paper, "Really?"

"Not mine."

"Oh, cool." He went back to reading.

"Fuck, I feel awful."

"Yup. Got run over, then put the truck in reverse and got ya again."

"Yeah, who was driving?"

"You were, always are." A saying we'd used for years for moments when we over did it the night before.

"Who's that chick?"

"Which one?"

"Apparently one I met last night. She hopped into the shower with me this morning. Hot, tan, nice tits."

"Zoe. That would be Robin's cousin."

"Who's Robin?"

"The girl I'm dating."

"The stripper?"

"Yup."

"Cool. Nice girls."

"Yup."

"Wish I could remember her. Seemed like she's fun."

"If you can't, you'll get to know her again."

"What's that mean?"

"She's staying here for the week. Her and Robin both. Robin's apartment flooded yesterday morning. So I told them they could stay here til its fixed back up."

"Interesting."

"If you say so."

"Well, I'm gonna go back to my place and get cleaned up a little better. Maybe write a little."

Again, the paper dips, "You gonna be okay?"

"Fine. You don't need to worry so much."

"But I do."

"That was three years ago. I'm okay."

"Alright, come back tonight. I still have some sweet dreamers left. I need your mind here to make them worth the investment."

I laugh, "Alright, I'll be back, won't be til later though. I really need to get some writing done. I already got the sketches outlined, so I just need to finish up the story."

"Can't wait to see it."

"Maybe I'll bring by the rough's tonight."

"Sweet, see ya' then."

I toss the rest of the coffee down like a shot of cheap whiskey, grimacing as it slides down my

throat. I get up and walk out of the house in a
hurry, wanting some clean pants. While walking, I
am finally able to focus and remember a little of
the night before. Which provides a welcome
distraction from this heat.

A warm Tongue from Eckry Mouth

Chapter Two

A warm tongue from a dry mouth lathered itself over my flesh, or at least it seemed. Humid summers in Fresno, fucking blessed be the survivors.

There I stood, on my balcony, staring across the street at the Japanese bar lit with neon signs shaping a name that I couldn't pronounce. A group of guys in their early twenties stumbled out into the early evening. They looked drunk, and were obnoxiously loud. I'm glad I was never one of those guys.

I heard a thud and scrape from the opposite end of the complex, I smile and mutter, "Fucking idiot." I know the sound too well, someone hitting the speedbump too fast, I can see the sparks flying

from the undercarriage in my mind. I shake my
head.

"Better get back to it." I tell the butt of my
cigarette before tossing it into the empty coffee
can sitting beside my plastic outdoor bench.

The house was hot, and I'm too cheap to run
the A/C. Not that I don't have the money. I just
like to keep the money. Sometimes when I shop, I
compare the things I think about buying, to the
things that I actually buy. So, I'll see a really
cool painting, see the price, and think, "Fuck, that's
like three bottles of whiskey and a carton of
smokes." Quickly dissuading myself from the
purchase, realizing I'd rather have the whiskey and
smokes.

I meandered through the living room,
procrastinating by convincing myself that there
were more pressing matters at hand. Looking over
the TV, I glance down at the PS3 tucked beneath the
glass entertainment center, decide against it.
Moving further, I flipped on the bathroom light.
Looked fine, Celia apparently came by and cleaned. I

could tell because my pile of clothes had been removed. Probably tossed into a hamper I wouldn't recognize even though it sat in my closet for months.

Finally, I give in and work my way to the spare bedroom that I had made my studio. Along the walls hung my sketches. I'd put them to paper about a month ago after a night of drinking and a lot of shrooms. The memory of actually creating had been beyond me, but there they sat the next morning, in a heap, in the middle of the room. With me passed out beside them, and the pastel stained fingers to prove I'd made the mess.

The story that held them together was still a little further down the road, apparently. I'd been stuck for a while, and I needed to get something out before I conceded and called it a block. But I refused thus far. Instead I'd begun forming a story about an angel I'd seen once, but hadn't much other than that to go on. Just monotonous characters through a very two dimensional story.

While looking down, trying to gather the patience to reread what I had for the story so far, I heard a knock at the door. It was Efren. Either he was having a party, or my sister wanted him to check up on me. Either way, it was a welcome distraction, and one I could easily blame on someone else instead of my own lack of discipline.

By the time I'd made it to the living room, my door was ajar, and Efren sat on my couch. He looked around burdened with boredom.

"Is there a problem?" I asked while walking to the kitchen so that I could grab a new pack of smokes from the cabinet.

"Well, being a story teller and painter, your walls have always bugged me. This house is so plain and bland other than your working room, and I just expect something more interesting to be up there. Like, I don't know, an angry angel skewering a puppy or a baby eating some brains. You know? Something just, fucked up."

"Sorry to disappoint you." I said sarcastically.

"Oh, it's okay. Anyways, get your shoes on, we're leaving."

"Helen?"

"Yup, been blowing up my phone all day. Says you've reached your alone time limit."

"Celia's coming by though."

"We'll call her and tell her to take a detour over to my place."

"You know that won't go over well."

"That makes it even better." He stood from the couch and lit a cigarette. He'd never been a fan of hers.

"Come on, man. You know she hates that shit in the house."

"Oh, she does?" He feigned surprise, "Well I had no idea. My apologies, I'll wait outside. Get your kicks on, let's bounce." He walked out, leaving the door open. I slid on my Chuck's and locked the door on the way out. I had a room at Efren's, so even if I got stuck there all night, I had whatever I needed already loaded in that room.

We hurried down the steps, hoping T.O., my neighbor, wouldn't hear us. He liked to tag along sometimes, but his wife was more a mother than a wife. She had actually come up to my place and scolded me for taking him out too late at night...twice.

I heard the two of them arguing as we approached the foot of the stairs. Efren heard as well, looked at me, then we bolted down the sidewalk towards the end of the block. Once we were about there we slowed to a walk.

Efren sighed, "Poor bastard."

"Yup. So what do you got going on tonight?"

"Party. But this one's special."

"Oh, really?"

"Yup, Robin is coming out, our first date."

"The stripper?" The stripper had been his life mission for the past two months since he'd seen her at a friend's bachelor party.

"The one and only."

"Cool. Look forward to meeting her."

"You could give a rat's ass. But thanks for pretending you give a shit. It means a lot, I know you don't do that for everyone."

"So sentimental, she must really have you in a sweet spot."

"Let's just get there. She probably made it to my place already."

Efren lived down the block and around the corner. It took less than ten minutes to get to the residential street where his house sat thumping loudly on the corner.

Changes by Bowie blared into the evening. It seemed to fit, as the sun was setting, the sky an orange and purple beyond the layer of smog above. We walked up the pathway that weaved through a rose garden, then up the few steps to the door. He opened it and entered, ushering me into a fog of weed and cigarette smoke. On the left was a living room with a double door entry way. Four guys with a three-foot bong helped each other out. You know, fucking team work. They looked over and nodded in greetings. I returned the kindness, but they'd continued on not really giving a damn who was coming in or going out.

Continuing on I glanced down the hallway that made an L, my room just around the angle, which was crowded with bodies holding red plastic cups. We turned right instead, into the dining room/kitchen. The floor was tiled, plastic fold up table set off by the sliding door that led out to the pool. A crowd stood around the table, while teams of two raged on amidst a game of beer pong that seemed to be coming down to the wire.

Efren bypassed that, and led me to the kitchen where he pulled four shot glasses down from the cabinet above his coffee pot. Reaching into the fridge he retrieved a bottle of Jack. Filling the glasses to the rim, he looked around and gave me a finger that said, "Wait." As much as my salivating mouth wanted the shot, I did so.

After leaning left and right, looking around desperately, he waved an emphatic arm in the air trying to signal someone. I didn't bother trying to find the target through the crowd, instead I watched him, thinking that he looked like a jackass right now. Finally, he stopped, with a shit eating grin on his face. I had the glass in hand, impatiently waiting to quench a thirst that was becoming quite the insatiable little bastard.

A woman I presumed to be Robin arrived. Bright red hair (obviously a dye job) and big tits threatening to spill out over a black dress that was covered in glitter. The black dress made her seem Casper pale, but she was attractive none the less. The short dress showed off her muscular arms and legs, kind of left me a bit worried about Efren. She looked like she'd break him with ease.

Behind her came the other girl. Her hair up in high, disarrayed pigtails, colorful, beaded bracelets and necklaces that looked homemade. Tanned skin and a petite build, she had this look of, "I'm gonna fuck you up." Just so pissed off, yet when she reached us, she smiled in a natural portrait sort of way.

"Who the fuck are you?" I asked from the straggler.

Hazel eyes looked up at me (she was a little on the short side), "Zoe. Who the fuck are you?"

"Ezra." I looked at Efren, "Who the fuck's this?"

"Robin's cousin."

I looked back down at her, she grabbed a shot and looked back at me, "We admiring these or gonna drink them?" She was starting to grow on me already.

We, all four, grabbed our shots and raised them up, "Lead us in the salute." Efren said to me.

"Slits, tits, and clits." My poetic offering was sent out to the night, we drank, and at that exact moment, I totally fucking forgot about Celia. No shit, just gone, wiped out, I was lost then. Although I didn't know it at that point.

Grabbing some beers from a fridge full of them, Efren handed them out. We walked passed the pong table, and right to the sliding door. Stepping outside, the sun had set, and the backyard was crowded with drunks in the pool, and some just standing around it. The four of us sat on the edge, removing our shoes and rolling up pant legs before dipping our feet and legs in. Kicking around the water we cracked the beers and sat in an awkward silence for a moment. Just judging from the seating arrangement, Efren beside Robin, Robin beside Zoe, Zoe beside me, I got the distinct feeling this was a bit of a set up.

I leaned over looking at Efren, he looked back, smiled that grin again, and then started talking to Robin. Zoe and I sat in an unsettled silence, watching our feet in the water.

"You guys hear they're finally making that Our New Bed movie?" Robin asked. I cringed. Efren got quiet quick.

"It'll be shit." I said.

"It won't be that bad. I guess Christopher Devereux helped write it. He would add a little humor, even if it is the dark sort."

I looked over at Zoe, feeling a little accosted, "Humor? Why humor? It was a sad fucking story. Why would they add humor?"

"Because it was such a downer. There was a moment of happiness, then just tragedy and death in a mudslide."

"So? That was the point of the story."

"Think of <u>Sling Blade</u>. Sad, yeah, but they added humor to make it more easy going on the people watching. Who wants to see a movie that leaves you feeling like slitting your wrists? I mean, you can't just bum people out for a whole hour and a half."

"But then you miss the whole emotion the writer was trying to convey. It was sad, he was ripped off. Life gave him the fucking finger. He wanted to give it right back."

"By killing himself? That's just giving up. He told a great story. The graphic novel is something I absolutely adored, but come on. As a movie it just wouldn't be the same, even with some of the visuals, it's just not something I'd sit and watch, personally."

"He had a story to tell, and he told it. Doesn't mean anyone has the right to go fucking with it."

Efren leaned over with a worried look, "Ezra, settle down man. It's just a movie." I nodded, realizing that what he meant was I was getting riled up and needed to calm down. "Sorry for losing my temper." I said to Zoe before getting up and walking back to the house. I bypassed the crowd gathered around the table and made it to the kitchen. Grabbing the bottle of Jack, I filled the shot glass and tossed it back, chasing it with three more. Capped the bottle, realized I left my beer outside, grabbed a new one from the fridge, not wanting to return to the sight of my outburst.

Popping the cap, I left the kitchen, stumbled through the dining room, then splashed into the hall. I crashed into sweaty, hot, clumsy bodies that couldn't sit still. Whether they wobbled or danced in the narrow hall, I somehow managed to bump into each one on the way to my bedroom. Fumbling in my pocket, I found the key, arrived at the door, unlocked it while shoving a drunken fool out of my way while he leaned against it, hitting on a brunette that was three scales out of his league. Just as the door swung open, a hand landed on my shoulder, shoving me inside. As I stumbled into the room, I heard the door slam shut. I heard the lock turn on the door knob. Looking behind me I found Zoe with a panicked look. A stood, regaining my balance, "What the fuck?!"

"You're him, aren't you!" she wasn't asking, she was accusing.

"What the fuck are you talking about?"

"I know you are. I could tell. You're him, fuck! Oh, my god, I can't believe it. I'm such a huge fan."

I turned and sat on the edge of a mattress that was tucked into the corner of the room. Pulling out a cigarette I lit it up and said nothing.

"Sorry." She takes a breath to calm herself, and then sits down beside me, "Didn't mean to go all fan boy on ya'. Just a bit of a surprise. You know, most your fans think you're dead?"

"What?"

"Yeah, your last few books were so different, they believe that someone else is writing them for you and just publishing under your name to keep it alive."

"What the hell. That's fucking stupid."

"Yeah, but, they have a point. Your stuff lately has been way different. Wasn't as dark as the first two, more adventure type stuff, less personal with the characters." I huffed, a little defeated. She was right. I guess they were right. Deflating, I drank from the beer and dragged from my cigarette.

"I didn't mean to corner you in here. Anger kinda got the best of me on the way over and I didn't really think, just reacted, you know?"

"Anger?"

"I don't know how to explain it. I just felt angry that it was you and you didn't tell us."

"Efren knows."

"He does?"

"Yeah." I laughed a bit, "He's been there since we were teens. Bastard's saved my life a few times. Literally and figuratively."

"He doesn't strike me as that type."

"That type?"

"The type that does anything but run with their tail between their legs."

"He would surprise you."

"Tell me."

"Well, we were at the river with some friends. Only around sixteen, maybe. We had been drinking for a while, swimming, just having a good time. My sister was there too with some of her friends. They were a bit older, they played a game called hangman, not the word guessing game. There was a train bridge that crossed over the river, they would climb up to it, walk to the center, wait for the train, climb underneath and hang on to the beams while the train crossed the bridge. Whoever held on the longest won. If you lost, you crashed into the river below. It was deep enough so that you didn't have to worry about hitting bottom. They played this often, my friends and I had never played, so they took us up with them." I pause to smother one cigarette, only to light another. I offered her one, she declined.

"Helena, my sister, oh she was pissed. She did not want me up there with them, but I was stubborn, like her, and went along. We sat up there drinking beer, waiting for a train. It took about a half-hour before we finally felt the tracks vibrating. We started climbing down, but we weren't quick enough, we didn't have time to really get a good grip. The train came, the beams underneath were shaking so hard, we couldn't hold on. Peter, Helena's boyfriend fell first, then his friend Thom was next. Then I dropped, I hit the water hard, I remember pain in every inch of my body; I thought I was paralyzed. I couldn't move, I floated to the top, and suddenly my arms were waving, pushing me towards the shore, but something had caught my leg. I turned back, Thom was thrashing around, he couldn't get loose. Peter had swum back to shore, laughing at us.

Helena was screaming, she finally jumped in and started swimming towards us. I yelled and yelled for her to stop, afraid she'd get stuck too. Some asshole had dumped off rolls of barbed wire along with some trash there in the river. Something becoming more common over the years. Disgusting, dangerous, and you couldn't see it there under the water.

"Efren fell in, he swam to me, dived under, I could feel him groping my leg, trying to work his way to the wire. I quite kicking, my body sinking slightly. Suddenly a relief of pressure from my leg, Efren popped up and we swam to Thom, we got him loose, but it was too late for him. When we get him back to shore, his body was gray, lips blue. We called 911, but he was long gone. Kicking with that wire around my leg had shredded it up pretty good. Twenty-three stitches in my leg. Still have the scars. After that though, Efren and I have always been friends. He hasn't saved me so dramatically again, but, he's done his part of watching over me, and has saved me from myself quite a few times."

"What happened to Peter?"

"Don't know, Helena never spoke to him again. I never heard from him again, and I never asked Helena."

"Wow. Your sister sounds like she loves you a lot."

"She does, for a long time all we had was each other."

"What about your parents?"

"Gone."

"Dead, or left you guys?"

"Not sure. Just vanished one day."

"Ever try to find them?"

"No, not really. If they are dead, then looking for answers won't bring them back, and if they left, obviously they didn't want much to do with us or they would have stayed. Helena and I did fine on our own. We don't need to dig into the past to discover who they were. We know who we are, and that is who we raised each other to be. That's enough for us."

"That's good. Things couldn't have been easy, but, sounds like you guys made the best of what you had to work with."

"I think we did pretty well." I finished my beer and tossed it in a small trash can underneath my writing desk. She did the same.

She stared into her clasped hands for a moment, "Are you ready?"

"Yeah, I think so." I smother my cigarette in the ashtray on the corner of the writing desk besides the bed, leaning the half unsmoked on the ledge of the tray. We stand and leave the room, back into the hall of human bodies. Making our way to the dining room, we found Robin and Efren playing quarters at the counter. We waited until they finished, then joined in on another round. After two more matches, everything starts to come in blips. I am talking to Robin, I blink, I'm talking to Efren, I blink, I'm talking to Robin. The transition was a bit troubling, but I just went with it. I'm sure it's occurred before, I just can't pin point it at the moment. Then, as if I wasn't fucked

up enough, Efren pulls a bag of Sweet Dreamers
from his pocket.

There's a dozen pills inside. He hands each of
us two, which is a lot for just one sitting, but, who
am I to judge. I chase mine down with a beer,
grabbing another one from the fridge afterwards.
The three of them go out to the pool, but I still
stand beside the counter. I stay to have another
drink, but then I see the angel. She walks
carefully around the bodies in the room. Making
her way towards me, her eyes are locked onto mine.
I'm in a trance, I can't look away. She begins to
shake her head at me, her mouth opens to say
something, but no sound escapes. Then she vanished.
Just gone. I look around the room, but no one else
has noticed her at all. Nausea strikes. Trying to be
as unnoticeable and casual as I could, I started
making my way towards the bathroom, thankful for
the miracle that it's empty by the time I reach it.

I shut the door and move fast to the toilet.
Dropping to my knees as I simultaneously lift the
toilet seat, I hunch over and start unswallowing.

After retching again, I push myself away from the seat, giving it a flush, and trying to catch my breath. A knock came at the door, "I'll be out in a sec." I yelled.

But the door opens anyways. It's Zoe. She shuts the door and sits on the floor beside me, "You okay?"

"Yeah. Just sort of, a mixture of everything I guess."

I rub my hands over my face, it tingles to the touch. She fills a glass from the counter with water from the sink and hands it to me. I swish a mouthful of water then lean towards the tub and spit it out. When I sit back up, she is closer now. She takes the glass and sets it on the counter top. I'm staring into beautiful hazel eyes, then her lips are pushing against my own. Her tongue dances its way into my mouth, where my own partners up and joins in. She's pulling me down on top of her.

The tile turns to liquid as her back splashes into it. My hands on either side splash into the cool aqueous tile as I brace myself. I see the ripples flow from under us, throughout the rest of the bathroom. Her fingers work at the button of my pants, eagerly trying to unlatch them. When she finally gets them loose, she works them down with her feet, refusing to let go of my mouth, or letting me move at all. She tugs hers down, grabbing my hard on and pulling it towards her with a tight grip. As I slide inside of her, I exhale, slightly making some strange noise I'd never recalled making before. As I begin to thrust, I feel her hands gripping my ass, I pull my mouth away just long enough to see her with a smile slightly crazed. I look down at our pelvises and find that we are melting into each other, our flesh melded together, connected, becoming one.

The bass from the stereo outside seems to become louder. I look up and see the blurs of sound waves traveling through the air. Her hands fly to the sides of my face and force me to look at her. Her body vibrated so hard at each thump that she seemed to split into two, more so each time. "Harder. Do it." So I did. I thrust hard, I wanted to fuck her in two. The sound, so loud, bouncing off the walls, the wetness, the skin tearing apart, reconnecting at each moment of contact, and then smacking into her thighs as I rammed myself in again. She opened her eyes and I saw stars. The night sky, so dark and infinite, and with it, stars, million upon millions. She raised her head from the floor, wet tile dripping off of her hair, making me look closer. Then she flung her head back, moaning loud, giggling in between breaths. The bathroom door opens, and she hugs me down tight on top of her, covering herself and leaving me bare ass out in the open.

Efren and Robin ran in, shutting the door behind them. They looked at us looking at them, "Sorry guys." Robin said while they stood there laughing hysterically, "Really gotta go though." She stepped over us, pulled her panties down to her ankles and sat on the toilet, pissing in front of the crowd.

Efren drank from his solo cup when he began looking around the room, then at the tile, "Whoa, who's having the cool trip."

"I believe it was her." I answered while I stood up, pulling out of her and working my pants back on.

"Well, let's go out and let you do one of your really cool shows."

"Maybe in a few, I need another beer first."

"Let's do it."

I looked down and caught a glimpse of Zoe's landing strip as she tugged her pants back on. She noticed, smiling at me, "Maybe later, lover boy."

We made our way out of the bathroom, Efren and Robin leading us through the hall, to the dining room, and then out to the pool. Five minutes later, we were floating around on air mattresses, Zoe and I on one, Efren and Robin on another. The party had started to thin, but a few people still sat on the patio talking, drinking, smoking. Zoe and I watched the stars, me just thinking of her eyes mostly, her, actually paying attention to the lights in the sky.

"Do it, Ezra. Come on, man. You haven't done this in a while."

I looked over at Efren, a little annoyed, but giving in. I closed my eyes, and started forming the picture in my head.

"He's the best at this. Sweet Dreamers are like, this guy's game. It's always either super twisted, or super cool. Either way, it's just plain ol' goddamn awesome."

I cast an evil eye at him, then decide on what we'll see. I look back up at the sky, and the others follow my gaze.

The stars began to move, shifting into a cluster. The girls gasped. Two forms began to take shape. A man, and a woman. They took each other's hands, and began to dance. They moved slowly, rhythmically. Twisting, swaying, around them a neon pink glow starts to spread. The stars around the figures exploded, turning to supernovas, and they danced in the middle of it all. Black rose petals rain, drifting down onto us all. Zoe picked one off of her hair, held it gently between two fingers, then examined it carefully. It would seem real enough, but that was only because I convinced her mind that it was. In all actuality, she held nothing but air, only I was aware of that in the moment though. The petals turned from black, to a bright blue, red, pink, and white. Slipping into the water, they began to melt, turning into neon paint.

Swirling together, quickly over taking the water, strands of paint like fingers began reaching out of the water and into the air, streaming into the sky. Weaving in between stars, circling around the dancing couple, and swimming in patterns that began to leave colorful tracers in the night.

Then gradually, the colors began to fade along with the fingers. The pink glow shrunk, becoming nearly transparent. I looked at the edge of the pool, where a large mound of paint began to rise from the surface. Soon a wall had formed about twelve feet high, spinning and twisting, flowing like a fountain. Then, as a wave, the paint washed over all of us, tossing us off of our floatation and into the pool.

I felt my feet hit the bottom of the pool, and shoved myself up towards the surface. When I broke through the top, and look around, I find the water is back to being water. The others paddle, heads just above the surface, the girls looking a little bemused and confused.

"It's gone." Zoe whispered.

"It is." I reply.

"That was cool."

"It was."

"We should do it again sometime."

"I'm sure we can arrange that."

When we'd made it back onto the patio, we found that we'd been locked out. We banged on the door for a while, but no one inside heard us. We tried the windows and found only the one to my bedroom was open.

An 'X' Between Her Tits

Chapter Three

As I enter the apartment, I can tell Celia has been here. The smell of her scented candles still hang in the air. I hate that fucking smell. If I wanted my place to smell like a goddamn pumpkin pie with cinnamon, I'd go buy a fucking pie and bake it.

I head straight for the bedroom, the only place she kept anything of her own. Scanning the room around me, I see drawers hanging open from the dresser, empty. The crap she had on the nightstand beside her side of the bed has been cleared, and as I enter the closet, I actually have space. I find myself feeling more relieved by the moment. *Had she really annoyed me that much?* Guess I'm just not a people person.

I should really write though. Standing at the border of my work room, I hesitate on entering, I examine the room. I'm looking over the drawings of the angel and remember that night so long ago when I'd seen her. A familiar rage begins to boil inside of me, I need to walk away. Keeping myself detached from those memories has gotten me this far, I'd like to keep up the trend.

From my kitchen cabinet, I retrieve a glass and fill it with water and ice. I chug it down quickly, refill it, and then drain it instantly once again. Placing the cup upside down on the edge of the sink, I go for my bottle of Jack and a shot glass. With Celia gone, I don't have to worry about the bitching. I light a cigarette (inside my apartment for a change), and fill the shot glass. I toss it back, fill up the glass again, toss it back, I repeat twice more. Grabbing the bottle and glass, I walk outside to my balcony.

The plastic bench is hot as my ass hits it. Even through the pants. Watching the cars below, I remember that day. That fucked up morning. Sitting in the car afterwards, covered in blood, tears, and snot in the hospital parking lot. I remember the taste in my mouth, a mixture of all of them, and I didn't give a shit. I just stared at the picture of the cabin on my phone, the place we'd never call home.

I'm not even using the shot glass anymore, just going straight from the bottle now. The rage is beginning to consume me, I'm trying to calm myself, but part of me doesn't want to. I want to be mad. I don't want to be sad or contained anymore. I just want to scream and break some shit.

I abandon the bench, grab the bottle, knocking the shot glass onto the concrete below. I hear it shatter, but ignore it, even as the glass crunches beneath my feet. I see her before I'm even all the way inside. The angel. She is sitting on my couch. She's wearing a black dress, it's short, high on her milky thighs. She looks up at me, with those blue eyes that glow, I'm frozen. Her fingers oddly bent at the knuckles, they rest upon a knee as she crosses her legs. The elastic straps that hold on her wings are crisscrossed over her chest, making an X between her tits. Her eyes are intense, but

sad at the same time. Her lips seem to tremble, her
heavy boots shaking at the end of those narrow
ankles.

"What are you doing here?"

"You need guidance."

"Guidance? I need a lot of things, but I don't
think guidance is one."

"You are lost; I will lead you."

"Lead me where? What the hell is going on?"

"You must make the journey. You have to go."

"I'm not going anywhere, you crazy bitch."

"You need help. You are blaming yourself."

"What the hell? I don't need help. What's
going on?!" I walk to the couch and stand over her.
She looks up at me, still frustratingly serine.

"She doesn't blame you. She blames herself."

"Who?"

"Annie."

reaction takes over, thought falls into the
shadows, I raise the bottle by the neck, and swing
it down. But when I should feel contact with her

head, the couch is empty and I'm falling onto the cushions.

"Helen needs your help."

I turn, she's standing behind me. Pushing myself off of the cushions, I stare at her, "What did you do to Helen?"

"Go to the sanctuary."

No one but Efren and Helen knew about that place. No one else knew I'd been there.

"She's stuck in the land between here and there. You have to be quick. And you're going to need the girl. She is instrumental for this journey."

I am confused, what girl. Not Alice, couldn't be Alice.

"Alice. Take her to the sanctuary. You will need her in order to bring Helen back."

"Where is Helen?"

"I must go." The wings on her back change. At first they just looked like cardboard with black feathers glued on. But before my eyes, they morph, growing six, maybe seven feet on each side, thicker, muscular, then begin to flap. Through my ceiling she propels herself. No mark in the sheetrock or stucco is visible. She'd just passed through like air.

Immediately I run to my cellphone. I dial Helen's number, I let it ring until it gets to her voicemail.

Not bothering to leave a message, I call Norman, her husband.

"Hello?" He sounds panicked.

"It's Ezra. Is Helena there?"

"Ezra. She's gone. I can't find her anywhere. She just vanished. She got into the car to go get Alice some food, then I found the car in neutral, backed into the pine at the end of the driveway. Still running, her phone and purse inside, I called the cops already. They said they'd be here soon to file a report."

"She's just gone? How is she just gone, Norman?"

"I hate to say this, but, it looks just like when your parents vanished."

My stomach dips, a hollowness inside of it. I hang up the phone, toss it on the bed, and walk back to the living room and pick up the bottle of Jack from the couch, there isn't a lot left, my greedy ass cushion soaked up most of it. Pressing the spout of the bottle to my lips, I tip whatever is left into my mouth, then, with the empty bottle in my hand, I turn and throw it as hard as I can into the TV behind me. Exiting the living room, I enter the kitchen and grab a new bottle from the pantry, my last one. Pulling the tab to tear the plastic, I twist off the cap and drink hungrily. I look around, wasted, all of this wasted, the apartment, the money, the skills, it isn't worth a shit if you don't have anyone. I'm robbed again.

Should I go? Do I listen to the angel? Alice, oh poor Alice. That poor child.

I wonder sometimes if Annie hadn't died, what would have come of us? I think sometimes of that first night together. Can't believe it's been six years. The time passes so quickly when I think back on it, but at the present, it feels so slow.

Running back to the room, I grab the phone
and call Norman back.

"Ezra, is everything okay? Is there something
I need to know?"

"Listen, this is gonna sound weird. But do you
know about my sanctuary? Did Helena ever tell
you?"

"Yeah."

"I need to take Alice with me there. I can't
really explain why; I just need you to trust me on
this."

"Ezra, do whatever you have to do. Just get
my wife back here, please." He sounded so desperate.
His voice made my eyes water just a bit.

"I will. I promise."

"I won't pretend to understand what's going
on. I know weird stuff seems to happen to you guys,
your family, but I also know Alice is safe with
you. You'd do anything for her, I've been a witness
to it for years. But are you sure? I just have to
hear it from you, are you sure this is what you
need to do?"

"I am. And it won't take long. A week. Her and Helena will be back in a week, I put my life on it."

"When?"

"I'm going to get the tickets tonight, probably leave tomorrow night or the next day. I'll let you know for sure later tonight. Just take care of the school and make sure you have a birth certificate or passport for her."

"Okay. I'll talk to you then."

I hung up, then shove the phone into my pocket. It felt awkward, like a badly timed boner while starring in the Christmas play at church.

Standing in my living room, I take it all in. I pull the bottle to my lips, then flick my cigarette out to the side of the room, nothing but filter. I push another between my lips, lit it, I've made my decision. I was uncomfortable with it, but I'd made it. Migrating to my room I pack a backpack I hadn't used in years full of clothes, grab my deodorant, toothpaste, toothbrush, then zip it tight. From the walls in my work room, I gather my sketches. I crumple them, one by one. When I reach the last, I pull my lighter from my pocket and light it on fire, then toss it back into the room. I walk out, light another crumpled piece of drawing on fire, and tossed it into the room. I do this with each, except the bathroom, fucking linoleum.

I walked through and made sure each had kept. They did. The carpet in each room burns like a wool sweater.

Slinging my pack over my shoulder, bottle in hand, carton of smokes stuffed into the back of my pants, I leave.

So, you may think this is a little fucked up. *What about the other people in the complex, Ezra?* Well, quite honestly, fuck 'em. Don't really give a fuck about them.

My Chuck's slap against the concrete steps hard, and I break into a run as I hit the walkway.

I'm in a run pretty much constantly til I get back to Efren's. I don't knock, I just walk in. I enter the dining room. Efren, Robin, and Zoe sit at the dining table passing around a pipe.

"We gotta go to the sanctuary." I tell Efren.

"Now?"

"Tomorrow, or the next. But we're going. You guys can come too, if you want." I direct at Robin and Zoe. They just look confused.

Efren looks at them, then answers, "Alright, let's do it."

"I'm buying."

"What brought this on?" Efren asks.

"Helena vanished like mom and dad. The angel came back. She said we gotta go, and we are bringing Alice with us."

Efren suddenly looked worried, "The angel?"

"Just trust me on this Efren. If you don't believe me soon, I won't fight when you decide to have me locked up."

He thinks for a moment, then shrugs, "Free trip, can't complain." He hit the pipe, then handed it out to me, "You wanna explain to them or shall I?"

chapter four

What's really in front of your eye's

MAY HAVE BEEN

The where echo

failing

THE Whole fucking

T
I
M
E

And you didn't Even Notice !?!?

You ever look around at a place you've seen a thousand times, but at that moment, it seems completely different? A new beauty has arisen before your eyes, and you are just fucking awe struck. I feel that way sometimes in this town. I hate it so much, yet here I am, lingering like an echo in the Mercer Caverns.

Efren and I sit at the riverside off of Millburn and Herndon. We haven't been here in a long while. It's where he saved me the very first time. We've been here more times than I can count. But still, it's this new beautiful scene I can't fathom witnessing before. The water tugging around the trees, the grass sprouting through the gravel and sand, unrestrainable. This whole area so uncontained, free to spread and prosper.

I remember coming back to Fresno once. Heading up over the Grapevine, and at that point you get the most real visual you can have of your home. From blue skies, looms this cloud of doom. I shit you not, pulling up over that last hill, if you look up at the sky, you see the exact moment a blue sky turns to shit. A big brown cloud of shit that just hangs off the sky like a turd on a cat's ass. Didn't really dawn on me til I was older, that's home, that's where I live, that big dank cloud, that's me right there.

But a place like this, you forget about it. Even if it's just temporary. I mean, really, isn't life just a whole lot of, "That's good enough for now"?

Unless you're some rich bastard, are you satisfied? If you are, should you be? Shouldn't we all want more? The ideal, the dream, how many of us are living ours? I get paid a bunch of money to do something I used to love but now hate, that's why I give it all away more than I spend it. Wouldn't you? Help someone else get where you want to be if you know you won't get there before you're laying six feet under and leaving your waste for someone else to clean up.

"What are we doing, Ezra?"

"Sitting at the river."

"I get that. Why are we leaving?"

"I told you why."

"I'm sorry, dude. You have to see it my way though, we've gone through this shit before, you went fucking ape shit. I'd walk you by hand back to sanity, but I'm afraid one day you won't want to."

"You think this was all in my head?"

"It's a little sketchy, you know what I mean? I want to believe you, and part of me does, I guess. Another part of me screams, he's there again Efren, he's on the ledge, stop him from jumping over."

"Guess we'll have to wait and see. Unless you want to take the steps necessary to stop me."

"I'm not going to have you committed, man."

"Trust me. This isn't my mind, this is what is happening. If I could give you anything else to go on, I would. I don't. I won't. Not until it happens."

"Until what happens?"

"Whatever it is I'm supposed to be a part of."
I pass the bottle of Jack to him. He sips at it then
cringes a little at the taste. I light a cigarette
and gaze out over the water, the way the moon
reflects off of the peaks in the current was like
fireworks. The shadows play tricks on my eyes, and
the sounds of nature make me slightly paranoid, and
I like it. I feel so alert and awake. The
stimulation was more than I'd had in a long time. A
feeling of dread still stained my heart, but change
was coming, I could feel it laying over me like an
uncomfortable blanket. After all of this was done,
things would never be the same.

"You know the cops are gonna be looking for
you."

"Yes."

"How are you gonna get out of here?"

"Scott Peals."

"From high school?"

"Yup."

"Didn't even know you still talked to that guy."

"Occasionally."

"How's he gonna help?"

"He's a pilot now. Got his own little puddle jumper."

"Does he know what's going on?"

"A little."

"And he agreed to help?"

"With a little monetary motivation."

"Jesus, Ezra. This is a whole new kind of fucked up, dude. I'm just gonna say this once, and not bring it up again. Be sure, because if not, you're fucked. Like, not in a good way, you are just gonna be fucked. Nothing any of us do can help you at that point."

"I know. Don't worry. I know what I'm doing. Chaos is my specialty."

"No, the art of self-destruction is your specialty. I've witnessed it firsthand. I'll support you and follow you til the earth caves in on itself. I'll never question. Just do me a favor, and this once, second guess yourself and think it over once more."

"It's done, Efren. There isn't any going back now. You don't have to come with. None of you do. Just trust me. This is what I have to do."

"Alright." He lets it drop, so we sit in silence, watching the water, listening to the sound of the night's heartbeats.

"Ezra, did you see anything else when you died?"

"Like what?"

"I know you saw the angel and all, but, was there anything else?"

"Like a tunnel with a light, all my loved ones, an open bar with a never ending supply of Jack?"

Efren laughs nervously, "Yeah, I guess."

"No."

"So what happens when we die?"

"I don't know."

"But you died and nothing happened."

"Maybe I was just a little dead." I say sarcastically.

"No heaven or hell. It's hard to imagine a nothingness after we die. Just an end to it all. I mean, I've closed my eyes at night in bed, and wondered if that is what it's like. Just nothing. I mean, can we still think? Do we dream at all for at least a little while? It's just hard to imagine it all just stopping. What do you think happens when we die for real?"

I looked around, taking everything in that I could before we left, wanting to remember this all. I knew I would never see it again. Somehow, I just knew.

"I think... I think we all go to Alaska when we die."

Tittle Paper Boy

Chapter five

I look into Zoe's eyes across from me, but I don't find the starry infinite abyss I'd seen the night before. Instead I find Hazel eyes that look used and betrayed. The flame already seems to be fading.

The air in the room is stagnant, dry, useless. We dropped the Sweet Dreamers almost an hour ago, the effects instantaneous as usual, but still I haven't taken a turn, just watching the others, which hasn't been very entertaining. A throbbing in the back of my neck is slowly creeping into my skull. Migraine. Got them when I dropped the Dreamers occasionally. In an hour I'd start puking, then the pain would intensify until I slept. If I slept.

"Alright, you're up Ezra."

I sigh. I'm not sure what to throw out there. I am dreading the onset of the migraine more than I was interested in the moment I am caught inside of. Standing up, I walk to the middle of the room, and then let my mind bounce around for a few seconds before beginning.

"Once upon a time there was a little paper boy, who lived in a land made of paper. Beside this paper existence was a painted world, with a little painted girl." The walls of the room are pulled away, disappearing in the distance. The strands of carpet lay flat, as if under a great weight, then melt together, turning to paper on one half of the room, and paint on the other.

"The little painted girl danced in a wooded land, to the beats of dripping paint from the leaves above. Content, and blissful to her own devices." The painted girl spins, and dances, weaving through trees and brush like a ballerina, graceful, smooth, rhythmic.

"The paper boy however, was all alone in a vastness of pale emptiness. He'd spent many moments watching the little painted girl dance, sway, twirl, and prance across her land. Envious and curious of her." The paper boy walks across the emptiness of his land. The scrape of his rounded feet dragging across the paper is loud, like chalk heavily pulling across a chalkboard. His head hangs until he reaches the border of the painted land. It raises as he peers at the painted girl. "Then one day, he chanced an approach while she danced along the borderline of their worlds. As he got closer, she stopped her dance and watched. She had never noticed him before."

Both beings stand at the lip of paint meets paper, heads tilting while examining each other. He watches the way her flesh and hair continually shift like running water, changing color as it flows over her body.

"Then quite suddenly the little painted girl stepped over to the paper world. Tracing fingers along every blank surface, bringing life to his world. He followed as she wandered through the emptiness, leaving a trail of trees, streams, shacks, and animals in her wake. Once she had covered every empty piece of paper, she looked around, taking it all in. Looking satisfied with her results, she finds she's quite impressed with herself. The little paper boy looked around, feeling overwhelmed with joy at this new and lively world. The little painted girl held out a hand, and he joined his with it." The two beings stand in the vibrant world, holding hands. Both appear to be jubilant, happy as they look over the land around them, full of life and greenery. No longer just a blandness that he had to traipse through every day. Looking back at each other, they know that the best part of all, is that they now have each other.

"But then it all went wrong." The land of paper began to wilt and crinkle from the moisture of the paint, "His world began to fall apart, and so did he." The paper boy looks at his hand, seeing the paint soaking into it. He steps back, and his hand disconnects from his arm, but still clings to the little painted girl. She gazes down at the material clinging to her, trying to shake it off. But the paper has begun to absorb her own hand. The paper falls away, and her hand along with it. The two look at each other, unsure of what to do.

"Soon the paper world began to fall apart." The land of paper begins to warp, bending, heavy from the paint. Tears form, chunks plunge into the darkness below.

"They tried to escape it." Both begin to run. They run for the painted world, but as the little painted girl crosses the border, the little paper boy stops. She turns back and finds him looking down towards his legs as they are crumpling while the moisture continues to ascend his limbs.

"The little paper boy realized, although he'd seen this wonderful world, he couldn't exist with her inside of it." The little painted girl swivels her head around in a panic, seeking an answer, but finds nothing. The little paper boy is down to his waist now, his good hand reaches out and pulls the little painted girl close. They kiss. They stay locked together until he is down to his neck in paint. When they finally separate, his head falls back from the weight of the paint, and her face went along with it. "Blindly she made her way back to her home in the woods. Unable to see him fall away into the infinite abyss below. There she sat, for many more moments, until her world dried out." The painted world dried, then begins to crack, breaking away speck by speck, until there is nothing left. Everyone is quiet as the walls return, the strands of carpet break free, and the flecks of paint vanish. I sit back down and see tears in the eyes of the others.

Efren shakes his head while wiping at his eyes, "That is some fucked up shit, man. Fucked up."

I open my eyes. The room is dim, without blinds, I know it's early. Laying in the crook of my arm, Zoe sleeps, breathing heavily, an occasional snore. Looking at the way the light cradles the room, something doesn't seem right. A reflexive pull causes me to tug my arms. I'm rising into the air of the room. Soon I'm near the ceiling, looking down at myself and Zoe. We look so comfortable, so natural. I push myself towards the wall, and as I try to stretch my feet towards it, I find there is no substance, instead I sift right through it.

I'm in the hall, I propel myself towards the bathroom. Once I make it there, which is a bit of a struggle, I hover in front of the mirror. But it isn't me. Instead a Mockingbird flaps wings in the reflection. For some reason it feels normal, easily accepted by my mind, even though part of my brain knows that it shouldn't.

I leave there, and shove right through another room. I hover a few inches from the ceiling, looking down. Efren lays on the floor, Robin sprawled along the bed. Her legs and arms spread wide. She's naked, the sheet just barely wrapped around her crotch. Her breast's hanging heavily to the sides, her stomach pouched with a slight beer gut, her arms and legs so muscular, looking tense and flexed, even while she sleeps.

Trying to get away from the image of her naked body, I turn and fly from the room. Back in the hall, I guide myself outside. As soon as I'm out

the door, I feel the sun beat down like a heavy
sack cross a mule's back. I push higher, higher,
higher. Soon I overlook the city, watching the cars
that look like ants over a mound. The towers
downtown that don't look so intimidating any
longer, the bodies that I can barely make out
moving along the sidewalks. Everything so small,
registering no impact from this view, at least not
on anything visible to my eye. We're just so small
on the outside. Just so fucking small.

Then she appears. I don't really see her; I
see the wings. Swooping down, I see a body fall. But
in her hands, the same person flays, swings, kicks,
screams. She rises, reaching my spot high in the
sky, she stops, person still in a panic.

"I am the collector. I am the arbitrator. I am
the scale between life and death. You are nothing.
Take my advice or don't. But when the time comes,
no matter who you bring with you, we all die
alone." At first, I think it's the angel. But now
that she's this close, it almost resembles Annie,
but not quite.

"We?"

She just smiles, then flies off with limbs swinging and screams dropping behind from her victim. *I don't want to see this anymore*, I think. Suddenly I'm falling, my wings go limp; I no longer have any control over them. I hear cars along the road, I hear voices talking about things that don't matter, I hear laughter, and I feel scared. As my body rotates, I find I'm staring straight at the ground. It approaches in slow motion, my wings whip through the air erratically. As the impact comes to cognizance, I go numb. I feel no pain. I think nothing of it. I just feel fucking numb. If this is death, it isn't impressive.

Then I wake up, Zoe next to me, and my phone ringing loudly beside my head.

Chapter Six

I'll eat you alive
feed off who you
are

And shape myself
around it
Then Become
Brand New

When you walk through the snow, you leave a trail for others to follow. Ultimately, aren't impressions our only lasting legacy? Shared laughter, profound silences that communicate more than words, generosity and selfishness, inflicted pain and a healing touch.

In the snow, the ones we love know to follow our footsteps, or to leave their own, secure in the knowledge that we will find them. One simply cannot walk alone. I was a slow learner, but after years of wallowing in my own mistakes, I eventually recognized that truth. Like a foetus needs its umbilical noose, we all need someone to tug us back from the great beyond we may sink into occasionally.

The knowing makes it worse, Annie used to say. And I believed her. I had no reason not to. In my eyes she was the light, the way, the day. And even though I appreciate the wisdom in her words, I must confess that she didn't get it quite right. Sometimes knowing makes it worse, but in this instance, it was the opposite. The impending doom we recognize gives us time to say goodbye, to accept the rightness or at least the inevitability of what is coming. Not knowing leaves everything with an ellipses of sorts. Anything is possible with that, but you don't know how serious or faint the threat is. You are unsteady, not sure how to prepare for what lies ahead.

I remember it was windy, that first night. It remains vivid for the simple fact it was my first winter outside of California. I'd never encountered such cold numbness across my flesh, never seen snow in person, and never walked over a frozen lake. As I walked down Ferry Street, crossing Front Ave, down towards Water Street, the wind pushed me. My feet glided across the ice covered sidewalk, my arms stretched out, trying to keep my balance as I laughed wildly. Laughter didn't visit me much back then, especially such a manic bout, utterly disregarding the passersby, who eyed me as if I was a mad man.

Water Street was a frontage road that ran along the Susquehanna River, you could take fifteen steps off of the sidewalk and be sinking your toes into freezing cold water. I'd done it more than once since I'd arrived here, just out of curiosity and for the sensation. The cold from the water sunk deeper like this. Not like a cold shower, or sticking your hand into and ice chest. No, this cold felt like ice injected straight into the bone. It ached, it throbbed, then every piece of meat and skin seemed to fall away, leaving me bare to the surrounding environment.

It was supposed to snow more that night, but by the time I'd gotten to water street, it rained. I walked down the sidewalk until I got to a bench just beyond the glow of Water Street's only streetlamp. An overhanging tree branch dropped chunks of snow around me, and rain made my clothes hang heavy and tight, but I did not feel cold. From inside my coat I pulled a flask full of whiskey. I take a few swigs, then twisted the cap back on, before lighting a cigarette.

I was glad to be out of California, leaving that world behind. My first graphic novel had just been published, and a lot of attention had been paid in my direction. It was a blessing and curse. I had to escape. Several drunken nights on the road behind the wheel, and I found myself in Danville Pennsylvania, the epitome of butt fuck nowhere. Two weeks in and not a single person had recognized me yet. Until that night.

The sound of rain drops plunging into the river radiated loudly into the air around me, drowning my thoughts in the white noise the steady impact created.

"Think you could spare one?" I jumped in my seat, caught off guard by the feminine voice.

I looked behind me, where a hooded figure lingered. Unable to see her face, I turned back towards the river, "No problem." I dug out another smoke from my pocket and handed it over. She pulled a zippo from her pocket, lighting the cigarette as she sat beside me.

"Sorry, didn't mean to scare you."

"It's all good. Just didn't hear you come up behind me."

"Rain's loud, can't really hear anything else. What you drinking?"

"Whiskey."

"Care to share?"

"Sure." I reluctantly handed over the flask. She took a sip, swished it around in her mouth impressively, then took another before handing it back.

"I'm Annie."

"I'm Ezra."

"I know."

I looked over a little quizzically, "How is that?"

"Saw you over at the Brews n' Bytes earlier. Recognized you from the picture on the back of your book. Then when I looked out my window" she pointed towards a duplex across the street behind us, "I decided I'd come out and spark up an intelligent conversation."

"This is intelligent conversation?"

"Not yet. But the good intention is there."

"Good intentions just weigh us down."

"So pessimistic."

"Point being?"

"And bitchy."

"Excuse me?"

"Just your way I guess. Don't take it personally. It's just who you are."

"You don't know me, yet alone who I am."

"I know better than you think."

"What the fuck are you talking about? You sound fucking crazy."

"You're here hiding out from the attention. You wanted to vanish and somehow had the bad luck of landing here. Here you are alone, drinking, hiding that gun tucked in the back of your pants. What are you going to do with it?"

I said nothing.

"That's what I thought."

I still said nothing.

"Don't worry. Do what you please, I'm not here to stop you. Definitely be a damn shame though, not seeing what that pretty little mind of yours comes up with next."

"Nothing there. Tank's empty. Everybody seems to be expecting something amazing, but I've got nothing." My eyes stay fixated on the ripples and splashing upon the surface of the river.

"It'll come. I'm sure of it. Stop looking at it as something that has to be done immediately. Just stop thinking. Then it'll come. It'll just plop into your head like a giant raindrop."

Six years later, her words would pop back into my mind from that night. Just plop into my head. Little did she know, the next one I wrote would be about her death, and my biggest seller.

"Listen, if you're interested, my place is dry. I also have more smokes and cold beer. Care to see it?" How could I say no to that?

We entered her duplex, cold and soaked. The living room was the first crevice of Annie's world I entered. White walls, lined with posters of neon butterflies and oversized mushrooms jumped out at me. Black lights were the only illumination through the room, no furniture, no TV, nothing else in the room. We passed through, her flicking a switch on the wall of the next room that lit up the kitchen and dining room in dim, yellow light.

"Have a seat." She pointed towards a plastic, circular table in the dining room. The top was covered in a turquoise linoleum that looked cheap and old. Four chairs rounded out the table, and not a single one matched. One of plastic, another of wood, a steel folding chair, and a canvas outdoor chair. I sat in the folding chair.

"Ahhh, yes, the folding chair. That is the chair Pierre would have chosen. Are you sure you aren't he, mister Ezra?" I hadn't thought of that book in years.

"If I'm Pierre, does that make you the lion?" She only smiled.

Grabbing a pack of smokes off of the counter, she approaches the table and I. She sat across from me in the wooden chair, handing me a beer and setting the pack of cigarettes on the table between us. "Hurry and finish the beer, that's our ashtray. I broke my only one last night." She looked over at a pile of glass on the floor besides the trash can, "And what a good one it was."

She chugged at her beer, then lit a cigarette. Beginning to fidget and act nervous while we sat in an awkward moment of silence, I finally spoke up, "So maybe me coming here wasn't such a good idea. I have no problem going, I wouldn't be offended or anything if that's what you want."

"Oh, no no, it isn't that. It's weird, and I don't want to creep you out."

"I'm not easily thrown off."

"Well, okay. Here it is. I'm not saying I'm struck with love at first sight. But I'll tell you right now, we're going to get married."

I almost spit the beer out of my mouth while I was still taking a swig, "Is that so?"

"This feeling I have. Can't explain it. But this feels right, you feel right."

Thinking on it, I guess I had felt oddly comfortable.

"I don't want to sound like an ass, but I always get what I want. And I haven't wanted in a long time. But right now, I want you. Do you have a problem with that?" A confidence and fierceness glowed in her eyes as she pulled away the hood from her head. Wet blond hair fell in thick strands around a heart shaped face. Thin lips smirked and blue eyes sparkled. Her eyebrows arched, and fingers tapped onto the shitty table impatiently.

I was quite taken, I admit. "Not yet."

"Not a great answer, but one I'll take." She stood up, walked to where I sat and kissed me. "Fight or scream, your ass is mine as of now." I said nothing as she wrapped her fingers tightly around my face and pulled me in for another kiss. Such passion flowed from her, a craving like an addict that I must admit made me feel like the most important person in the world at the moment.

A little over a year later, we lived in
California, and were expecting our first child.

Bigger on the Inside

I'm looking down at myself in a puddle. Ripples roll over the surface, the rain distorting my reflection. I smell Spruce trees, I smell wet soil, I smell rain. My sneaker is partly sinking into the mud, my other safely atop the rocks in the gravel. Lifting my gaze, I begin taking in the scenery. The trees, the bushes, the roads, driveways, everything is in black and white.

"Been a long time, stranger." I turn around, and there she is, "I've been waiting. I'd like to say for the right moment, but, there never is one, is there?"

"Annie?" The name comes out a whisper from me.

"I knew you'd make it back eventually. But why did you bring Alice?"

"The angel told me to."

"The angel hasn't been to you. I know she hasn't. Not since the day you died. I know because I sent her in the first place."

"She said I had to come. Someone took Helen, I had to bring Alice because she will lead us to Helen. There was no other way."

"Ezra, oh Ezra. What have you done?"

"I don't understand." I pleaded. Color bleeds back into the world, slowly, crawling across the screen of my view. The green in the trees, the brown of the mud, the grey and white of the gravel. But as the color spread over Annie, she didn't look right.

Her hair was white as snow, her skin a strange mix of blue and grey, and her eyes, those once beautiful eyes, now filled with pools of blood. As she moved, and the rain began to calm, I heard the sounds her body made. Almost a rubber on rubber noise as her skin flexed and fluctuated with her movements, a rubber band snapping as each joint changed position.

I took a step back as she took one forward. She paused, "What's wrong?"

"Nothing, just stay back. Why are you here?"

Her hands held out in front of her, she examined them, then the rest of her body. The black tee shirt, torn denim jeans, steel toe boots, "Oh, god. I'm so sorry, Ezra. I didn't think about... I'm sorry, don't be scared. Please, it's still me. I swear it is."

The light from overhead suddenly dimmed. I look up to find a thick layer of clouds falling onto the sky, quickly blocking out the sun. She noticed as well, looking up, mouth agape.

"What did you do?" I ask.

"Nothing, this isn't me. This is what you've set into motion Ezra."

"What do you mean?"

"Oh, Ezra. Alice is so much more important than you realize."

"I'd never let any harm come to her, Annie. I'd give my life first."

"You wouldn't intentionally, and she isn't the one I'm really worried about, you are. There are others that may be trying to manipulate you, and her. There's a much bigger game at play than you realize. She has a lead role, and you, I am afraid, do not."

"I'll die? Is that what you mean?"

The rain started falling harder, pelting against the top of my skull, crashing into the ground, an impact so hard that it was beginning to drown out the sound of the world around.

"I miss you so much, Ezra. I wish I could tell you more. I wish I could do more. But this is your journey, it has already been mapped out, and there is no deviating from the course that has been set. Oh, my." She was watching the sky, a grin crossing her face. "You've got quite the mind my friend."

I looked up, seeing the clouds parting slowly, a red light beginning to break through, "What are you talking about?"

"The end of the world, it's about to take us. But you're envisioning it."

I continued looking up, watching the red light wash across us. "I'm not doing this."

"Yes you are. You just aren't aware of it. The minds a tricky thing."

She moves closer, and while she did, her body began changing. It was more lifelike, less elastic than before. By the time her hands were wrapping around my bicep, she felt like she used to. Soft, smooth, warm.

"Just watch. This is how it ends."

"For me?"

"No. But for most of the others. Not all, but most."

"How do I go?"

"Can't tell you that. But, it won't be anything like me. Won't be anything like when you tried last time. Although, you'll have a lot more guilt."

"That isn't possible."

"Wasn't your fault, Ezra. What happened to me, there was nothing more you could have done."

"I beg to differ."

"Think whatever you want, my path was set. I wish it hadn't been, but it was. Hold me. Please?"

I couldn't resist, I did. Her weight leaned into my chest, my arms wrapping around her, her heartbeat thumping into mine. "Isn't it beautiful?" she asked as the sky erupted into flames. I could hear a rush of water. It sounded distant, just faint, but was growing louder. Closer. Soon it was running through the trees across from us. It only swallowed us ankle high at first. "This is the way the world died."

"Died, like it already happened?"

"Things work different where I am now. But yes. To me, it has already happened, in a thousand different ways."

"There is a way to stop it?"

"There always is. But this one, it isn't for everyone. This one, it's just for a special few to survive. The story of our world is so much more than what we can comprehend. And that's fine, Ezra. We have to accept it as that. Something bigger than us."

"But maybe I'm bigger on the inside." I muttered as lightning split the sky, piercing the clouds, with thunder quickly rolling in behind.

I heard cries from the neighbors, I looked around more closely. I was at the cabin. My cabin. My sanctuary.

On the porch, I stood, with Efren, Robin, and Zoe standing close behind. I was unlocking the door. Then she showed up, Alice, coming up behind everyone. She turned her head, as if she was looking right at me. Something in her eyes, a recognition, she wasn't surprised to see me, even though the others could not. Then she looked away, like she'd never seen me.

The flames from the sky seemed to be reaching downwards, specifically towards us, the rest of the world seemed to be caught in a haze. The heat singed the hair of my head.

"Wait for it." Annie mumbled into my ear. I heard a rumble in the distance, the ground began to vibrate. The flames recede, and then it was just her and I. She looked into my eyes, "Love her. She ends with you. Love her. Because she is the last you'll ever love." With her soft hand, she pushed my face back towards the trees across from us. A shadow surged across the horizon, swelling above the treetops, building skyward. A wall of water, a tidal wave, whatever you want to call it, smashed into us.

My feet were thrown out from under me. Near my side, a limb from a tree stuck out, I tried to grab it, I overreached and my forearm caught instead. My arm bent back with a loud snap, but I didn't make a sound. I twisted in midair, my legs kicking over to the left, yet my upper buddy caught on the limb twisting me right. The current pushing passed, shoving my feet off the mud that I'd felt on impact.

Annie was gone. Hadn't even felt her slip from my arms. Looked around, and there was no sign of her, while I held on to the root of a tree protruding from the gravel. Little balls of fire started to fall from the sky. While I was pushed under the water, I could still make them out from underneath, raining down upon me.

A distant memory of my mother. She's cradling me in her arms. Her soft voice singing into my ears. The song is lost to me. But her grip on me, her affection, I can't remember such an unexplainable feeling. Her eyes peering down at me, that smile, that wonderful smile. Like no matter what I did, all was forgiven. That was the last thing I saw as the world ended. Everything went black afterwards.

I opened my eyes, sticking the key into the hole of the door knob. As I wiggled it, I looked back, seeing Efren, Zoe, Alice, and Robin. Then, passed the porch, and the trees nearby, in the driveway, near the road, I saw it. Annie and myself talking. A flash of lighting overhead, the crash of thunder, the crack of a tree splitting as it fell over, the wind shoving through leaves. When I looked back, Annie and I were gone. Alice was looking up at me, a smirk on her face, as she walks by me and into the cabin.

It's Their fault

Chapter Eight

"What do we do now?" We'd been sitting in this musky cabin for three days, trying to find ways to keep Alice entertained, ourselves from going crazy in the small barracks, while keeping an eye out for anything unusual without being paranoid.

I offer Efren the only answer I have, "I don't know." The floorboards over us creak loudly, Alice was up.

"I got it." Zoe said, she stood from the table we sit at and briskly climbed the stairs to the cabin's only bedroom. Zoe and I had been sharing it with Alice, while Efren and Robin slept on the futon downstairs.

"How long are we going to wait?"

"You guys don't have to stay here, Efren. I'm fine with Alice, we'll wait until we figure out what we're supposed to do."

"We aren't going to leave you. But we need to have a plan, something to do, something to push ahead. We can't just sit and wait for a sign. Go over it all again, there has to be something we're looking for."

"I have, over and over. There's nothing. I'm sorry, I don't know how else to say it, *this* is what we're supposed to be doing, it's just a waiting game."

From above we heard Zoe yell, "Guys, you should get up here, now!" We all abandoned our chairs and ran up the stairs.

In the dimly lit bedroom, Alice and Zoe stand at the window looking out towards the yard.

"What is it?" I asked.

"Just come look." Zoe ushered me in between her and Alice. The scene below was unsettling, somehow out of balance and wrong. A thick mist hid the ground, bathed in the light of a dying moon, its troubled surface undulated as though stirred by the passing of sightless, boneless, scuttling creatures. I could not imagine stepping into it without being hauled beneath its surface.

"You guys wait here, Efren come with me." We leave the room; the others remain standing motionless at the window. Hurrying into the kitchen, I reach into the cabinet above the stove and remove a black box. Flipping it around, I roll my thumbs over the combination wheels. The latch flips up, I pull away the cover to reveal a blue steel Walther .22 pistol and a box of shells. I know the weapon was loaded, but I checked to be sure.

"What the hell are you expecting out there?" Efren asked, suddenly uneasy.

"Not sure. Under the sink is a Maglite, grab it." I walk to the wall near the fridge and turn on the outside lights. I'd installed flood lights on all sides of the cabin last time I was here. Also hanging from the trees were surveillance cameras, but I'd never finished installing them unfortunately.

Peering through the door glass, the front porch looks clear. "Stay behind me." I cautiously open the door, the night chill bit deep, like an icy blade. I ignore it as best I can, stepping out, scanning right and left, my finger on the Walther's trigger. I can see maybe fifteen feet in the floodlight's glare, beyond that, misted shadows devoured the light. The car was gone as well.

"Shine the light into the trees over there." I pointed to the right. Efren turned on the light and narrowed the beam while aiming it. Nothing but darkness. No trees, no ground, just darkness. "Ahead of me." I order. Again, nothing but darkness. "Back inside." Efren retreats, holding the door open as I back into the cabin, never taking my eyes off the yard in front of me.

He shut and locks the door as soon as I step inside. "In the closet there is an extension cord, grab it." As he did that, I pull the fridge away from the wall. Pulling the plug loose, I scoot the fridge in front to the door. Efren hands me the cord, I plug the fridge back in and step back, looking around the rest of the bottom floor. Two more windows and nothing to cover them with.

"Inside the bedroom, there's a small attic space over the doorway, a small wood cut out is nailed over it, it isn't very sturdy. Inside is another gun, grab it and come back down here. Send Zoe down as well."

"Okay." Efren takes off, his eyes wide and scared. It struck me for the first time that I was responsible for bringing my friends into this and that I might not be able to bring them all home. So why didn't I feel guilty about it. Instead I just thought, *they wanted to come, it's their fault.*

A few moments pass before Zoe reaches the foot of the steps, "You and Robin flip the mattress over the window in the bedroom, the box spring over the other window at the top of the stairs. You guys stay up there, Efren and I will keep an eye down here. We just have to make it til morning."

She tries to nod, but instead makes a weird jerk of the head. "It'll be okay, Zoe." I tell her.

She repeats the motion with her head before running back upstairs.

"Got it." Efren said as he came down the stairs.

"We can move the entertainment center with the TV over to that window, then we only have to worry about the one on the side here. Give me a hand with it." I walk over and set my gun down on the top of the console after switching the safety back on. Efren grabs the other side, I reach down and unplug the surge protector from the wall, then lift and place the console right in front of the window. It covers all but the top three inches of the glass. "That'll have to do."

I retrieve a beer from the fridge and sit on the futon, watching the last uncovered window. Efren joins me, clutching a beer of his own, "Now what do we do?"

"I swear to god, if you ask me that again, I'm gonna crap on your face while you sleep. If I fucking knew what to do, we'd be doing it, don't ya think?" He says nothing, just nods with a dazed look on his face and his eyes glued to the window. Then came the knocking. The fucking creep factor in this situation was uncanny, I felt like I was in Silent Hill. The sound came from the door, behind the fridge.

I stand up and walk to the fridge, "Who is it?!"

"A friend of Ariel."

"I don't know an Ariel."

"The angel. The fucking angel." I turn and look at Efren who has the gun pointed at me.

"What the fuck are you doing?!"

"Shit, sorry." He lowered the barrel.

"Watch what you're doing, goddamnitt." I pull the fridge away from the door, "Keep me covered. Not shooting me if all hell breaks loose would be much appreciated, on a side note." As I peek through the glass, a strange looking man peered back at me. I open the door, stepping in the doorway to keep him from crossing the threshold.

"I'm here to take you to Helen." His long black hair was stringy, dingy looking. He was thin in a sickly way, his clothes seeming to barely cling on, taller than I by almost a foot. Had to be almost seven feet tall.

"How to I know that?"

"Well, I could have easily gotten into your cabin, but I chose this way instead. I thought it would be more polite."

I turn to Efren, "Whaddya think?"

"I think I just shit my pants." I glare at him, he sighs, "I think I don't want him in here, but we've been waiting for something to happen and here it is."

I turned back to the man, "Come in."

"Thank you." I step back from the entryway and let him enter. He doesn't look around or say a word, just walks to the wall behind the futon. Balling up his fist, he knocks firmly against the wall. He waits while tapping a foot impatiently, then knocks again. This time a knock from the other side replies. He begins knocking in a circular motion in the wall, about a foot in diameter, then steps back. A small hole appears.

Only the size of a pencil at first, but gradually growing. "Get the others." He sounds annoyed. I motioned for Efren to head up the stairs.

"Is there anything we should take?"

"No."

"Where are we going?"

"Where I take you. Where you need to be."

"That's vague."

"That's the truth." The hole was now around eight feet round, and on the inside was a shadow of what looked to be a giant.

"What's that?"

"Who. And that is a friend. Don't worry, he won't bite unless you give him a good reason to." The man smiles at his own words.

"What's your name?"

"Vincent. Don't bother remembering it though. We won't meet again. Follow us." He steps into the hole in the wall just as the others were heading down the steps.

"Alice, hold my hand, sweetie." Zoe tells her. She does as told. It was just then that I notice her demeanor. Calm, unmoved by anything that was going on. Like none of this was the least bit strange or unexpected. I brush off the thought and step into the hole after Vincent. It is cold, but not near as outside was. Nothing is visible but Vincent and the shadow that I can barely make out.

As the others enter, the hole behind us shrinks to the size of dime, then winks shut. We were thrown into darkness for a brief three seconds before a torch was lit. The shadow then becomes completely visible. The beast before us is covered in purple fur, with black horns that curled around the sides of his head, large hands with thick nails at the ends of each finger. I hear the sharp intake of breath as my friends took in the creature before us. I keep walking, as strange as it was, I didn't want them to see me bothered with it, just have to keep moving.

A light up ahead shone brightly, Vincent and the beast stopped, "You and your friends must go on alone. We cannot enter this realm. There is someone waiting on the other side for you. Just stay together and you will all be fine."

Vincent reaches out and grabs my arm, waiting for the others to pass me by, "This is a dangerous journey. You should not have brought them. What happens to them is no fault but your own now. Remember that." Then he steps back with the beast and melted into the shadows. I catch up to the others just as they are reaching the light. We all stop at the borderline, I lead the way, taking Zoe's hand, and pushing through what feels like a pool of water. I shut my eyes, feeling the liquid resist my each and every step, then it is gone. I open my eyes and look back to find Zoe and Alice right behind me.

"Ezra? Oh, no." I turned to see who was speaking, and there stood Helen.

Chapter Nine

Where The Hell Am ?

How The fuck
Should I Know?
x

My conversation with Helen would have to wait. I find us clustered in a narrow alley between towering brick walls. The alley stretched a hundred yards to our front and rear, funneling my attention to the figure of a man at the mouth of the alley. Thunder cracks as fire flashed from the gun in the figures hand, the bullets rocketing towards us.

I turn to the others, "Run!"

Helen pushes me back, just before wrapping herself around Alice. I'm stumbling backwards and looking at Zoe, whose eyes are wide, her face full of confusion. I hear a shot echo off the walls, then feel the splash of warmth land upon my face as a gout of blood erupts from a hole in the temple of Zoe's head. Putting my hands behind me to stop my stumble, the wall provides no support. Instead I fall right through it, my ass slamming onto a carpeted floor of a dimly lit bedroom.

For an instant, I lay there stunned. Touching my face, my hand comes away wet with blood and fragments of bone. Pushing myself back upright, I ran to the wall I'd just fallen through and placed my hands against it. Pushing was pointless; the wall had solidified. Examining my surroundings, I spotted a door beside a small bed. Without thinking, I charge through it, finding myself in a hallway. I head to the left, into a dim, candle-lit living room. Beyond it I see two children, a boy and a girl, sitting across from their parents at a table in an informal dining room.

They gnaw viciously at chunks of meat held in their bare hands, even though sets of utensils lay next to their plates. Behind them is a window, the only exit I need. I sprint towards the glass at full speed. Before I can anticipate the speed of his movement, the man has dropped his meat, leapt from his chair, and with strong arms, wraps me in a bear hug. My legs kick at the air as he slams me onto the ground, with his full weight landing on top of me.

The air from my lungs evacuates, somehow we are on our sides, him still holding me in the hug. I fling my head back, hearing a smack at the contact of my head and his face. His grip loosens slightly, just enough for me to get an arm loose, raise it up and spin, driving my elbow into his jaw. I see his face for the first time, pale, gaunt, eyes sewn shut, ears cut from his head, a stubby tongue protruding from his maw, blackened and pulsing like a leech as he groans and growls at the contact.

I was free from his grip, but just as I rise, the woman is upon me. Her nails dig into the flesh of my cheeks as she grips on tightly, trying to straddle me and pin me down. I roll, pushing all my weight into the motion, flipping her off of me and onto the ground. Using the table to hoist myself back to my feet, I spot a steak knife and grab it.

Sudden pain in my ankle. I look down, and the little boy has sunk his teeth into what little meat is there. I drive the knife down into his temple. He goes slack jawed instantly. With my hand still on the handle of the knife, I use my other hand around his head to lift him up and slam him down on the table, yanking the knife from his skull as quickly as I can. I turn and find the man is back up and charging at me, then from the corner of my eye I see movement. The little girl has jumped off one of the chairs and is in mid-air, en route to me. I hold the knife out blindly, hoping it catches something. I feel the weight as it plunges into her chest.

Her body folds awkwardly, her limp legs swing so high they nearly kick my face. I grab one, let go of the knife and spin. Gripping tightly to the leg, I swing her into the man's skull. Her head cracks like a melon as it collides with his. Dropping to the ground in a heap, the man no longer moves. I release the little girl, and look down to find her face has the same afflictions as the man does. She looked maybe six or seven. Who would do that to a kid?

The woman crawls across the floor, keening as she cradles the little girl's broken body. I didn't stay to watch, I couldn't. Monster or not, I'd just killed a couple kids, and although I didn't really have a choice, it still felt wrong. I shove the pang of whatever the hell I was feeling deep down inside with everything else I was unaware of feeling. I run to the window and kick at it. My shoe punches through the spot of impact, but the window doesn't just shatter like in the movies. It was at this point I realize two feet left of the window is a fucking door. Winning at its finest.

Yanking my foot back through, I unlock the door and run out.

I find myself in a cross between Tower District and the French Quarter. Neon lights pulse as if dancing with the darkness. Music crammed into small rooms, burst through hollow doors, bodies sway and stumble down the sidewalk, voices raised high, loud, singing and talking over the gabble of night-speak.

"Where the hell am I?" I ask myself out loud.

"Shadows Tale."

"What?" I turn to find someone standing beside me.

"Shadows Tale, that's where we are." A snow man, his pipe burning something that surely wasn't tobacco, and beady pebble eyes, stands there looking out onto the strip of bars, restaurants, theatres, and shops along with me.

"Where is it exactly?"

"The land between dead and way passed dead."

"I'm not dead though."

"You sure about that?" Then he slathers off down the sidewalk, a deep chuckle falling behind his path.

"Come in here, I'll get you a drink and break it down for you." I look over my shoulder, where an open door led into a bar. At the door stands a pretty blond with big tits that looked like trouble wrapped up in a tube top. I shrug, fuck it, didn't know what else I was supposed to do at this point. I really had no damn clue how to find the others yet. Bar to me meant safe zone in this foreign place.

I enter the bar, finding dirty green walls, wood floors that are cracked and sticky with liquor. However, I find the leather padded stools are quite comfy. As I lean onto the counter the blond walks behind it and asks, "What's your poison?"

"Whiskey, straight."

"Nice." She reached down and grabs a glass, setting it on the counter before turning to retrieve a bottle of whiskey, "Any preference?"

"What do you have?"

"Whatever you want."

"What's the price?"

She laughs, "There is none. Money has no place here."

"In that case, Johnny blue."

"Coming right up." Reaching into a cabinet, she pulls out the bottle and cracks it open leaving me a little awe struck. She fills the glass and slid it in front of me. Then she finds another glass, and pours some in, "To the infinite abyss." She raises the glass and taps it against mine.

"Infinite abyss?"

"You used that term in one of your books."

"You know who I am?"

"I do."

"How?"

"Long story. I'm Dee, by the way."

"Well, Dee, I'm a bit lost." I sip from the glass. The whiskey slips down smooth.

"You have no idea. You shouldn't be here. You aren't dead."

"So how come I am? Why is my sister?"

"Well, how did you get here?"

"Vincent."

"Oh, that's not good."

"Why is that?"

"Think of Vincent as a mercenary of sorts. Instead of being paid to kill or destroy something, he is paid to bring in people that aren't meant to be here. Unfortunately for you, if you aren't supposed to be here, the constable doesn't really care about that."

"The constable?"

"The enforcer here. Him and his posse of souls that answer only to him. Think of them as cops, and to them, you are a criminal on the most wanted list."

"So how do I get out of here? We were in an alley, then I got pushed through a wall while someone was shooting at us."

"The shooter was probably the constable. The alley, it was lined with brick, the openings seemed far away?"

"Yes."

"It's the crossroads. It leads to different parts of town. The walls are real, and illusion. There are breaks in it, and other parts, well, they're as solid as they seem."

"How can I find my friends? I have to find them and my sister."

"Chances are, they're dead already. If they aren't, I really have no idea how to find them. Think of this place as infinite. There are so many possibilities, it's a needle in a haystack. But I can ask around."

"Thank you so much."

"I wouldn't get my hopes up though. The constable is a bloodhound, it's rare someone escapes him."

"I know at least one of my friends are dead, but the rest were still very much alive last I saw of them."

"Sorry about your friend."

"Don't be. In all honesty, it didn't really bother me." Saying it out loud really hit like a punch in the gut. But it's true. It sucks that Zoe's dead, but it didn't have some sort of mournful effect on me. Then again, part of me knew she was nothing more than another distraction. "Sounds fucked up I guess."

"We are all broken in one way or another. Don't guilt yourself into feeling for her." Almost like she'd read my mind, "I'm gonna make my rounds for refills. I'll ask around while I'm at it. I'll be back in a few. Feel free to help yourself." She slides the bottle over to me then walks away. I finish my glass and refill it. There is never a good reason to pass up free whiskey. Especially whiskey this good.

Dead with A Heart Beat

Chapter Ten

As I sit watching a fox fucking a dwarf in the corner of the bar, I determine that regardless of what happens in the end, this is where I belong. Any inhibitions I'd once had were quickly fleeting. The fucks I gave, dissipating in the air before my eyes. The others were a fading afterthought. A spell had been woven in a flirtatious web that seductively lured me in, leaving me with no desire to struggle against its strands.

"Get it! Get it! Get it!" The dwarf screams in a high pitched voice. I find myself laughing loudly, but they don't care, they don't even seem to notice I'm here.

The door to the bar opens, and in walks a skeleton wearing a top hat, blazer, and nothing else. "Hey, Bo! Heard Ariel turnt ya to dust again!"

"Oh mon ami, she jus wanna reason to touch all she can't have, yeah. I be back, again and again, I be back, don' yooo doubt that no, no." He struts with a hop in his step, before he sits in the stool beside my own. From inside his blazer he extracts a pack of smokes, "You mind?"

"Not at all." I reply before beginning to quickly frisk myself for my own pack, finding that I lost them somewhere between here and the cabin. "Think I could get one of those, I seem to have lost mine on the way here?"

"No no, not et all." He slides the pack to me with the lighter on top, "They think turnt to dust is de end. Oh, but no no. We all dust, yeah, we all juz dust. You know?"

"I honestly have no fuckin clue what you're talking about." I say while lighting one of the sin sticks.

"One day, yeah, you mark 'em words, yeah. Dust, we all turn to da dust. Imma Bojangles."

He extends a boney hand towards me, "Ezra."
I shake the hand, regretting it. The touch was
gross, cold, felt a lot like hugging a rough toilet.

"Pleeeezzzed to make de acquaintance,
monsieur. You knew to de land, yeah?"

"I am. Just arrived."

"Too bad, yeah. Nuthin like the livin, but the
dead is good, yeah. Like party party and no good
thought to tell you no."

"Yeah." I had no idea what this bastard was
on about.

"Lemme!" He spotted the bottle beside my
hands. He took it and my glass, filling it to the
brim, then downed it instantly. Traversing through
his mouth, it drips along his spine and ribs before
puddling onto the ground beneath him. "Oh, good
good, that is. Yeah. Eh, you ever seen de ocean
touch da sky?"

"What?"

"You ever seen de ocean touch da sky?"

Thinking on it, I guess I had. A beach trip
Helen and I had gone on back in the late nineties.

We'd driven down to Carlsbad, a late night, last minute idea of a trip. With a case of beer passing between us, somehow we'd gotten there alive.

Parking on the curb of the street, we jogged through the sand, charging towards the ocean. We dove in, the water cold as fuck. Running back out, we walked the beach and talked for about two more hours before laying with our heads propped up on a log that'd washed ashore. The sun was just starting to peek over the edge of the world when we fell asleep.

We slept for damn near seven hours before waking up with one hell of a sunburn. Our faces were scorched, cracking and leaking a clear liquid when the skin was stretched anything more than stationary.

That evening we sat on the beach, eating burgers and sipping on Chartreuse while watching the sunset. Just before the sun touched the sea, the sky and water melted into liquid gold. Like paint blended on canvass, the horizon vanished in a seamless wash of color, but without the clumsy artifice of human thought. Then with a final flare of orange and purple, air and water parted once more. "Yeah, yeah I have."

"den you know what izz really like, da world round us and all."

"What do you mean?"

"All connected, yeah. All one even difren' it still da same, yeah. Can't trust your eyes." Two boney fingers pointed at empty sockets in his skull, "No no, jusss layers dat overlap try and hide what really sits below."

"What the hell?"

"Trust me, yeah, all is not it seems, no."

With that, Dee walked back behind the counter and grabbed the bottle from him. "Stop being crazy Bo. Leave the newb alone." She shook her head at him before her gaze returned to my own, "I got word some strangers were heading towards Blight's Orchard."

"How do I get there?"

"Pretty easy, I'll show you. 'bout to clock off, so just give me a sec."

I finished my smoke and slid off the stool,
Dee reappeared and grabbed my hand, "Stay close."

We stepped outside as a car sped by, its tires
trailing a spray of cold mist. I looked more closely
at the cobblestone surface. Ripples ran through the
stone, I knelt and placed my hand on the road. My
hand dipped into liquid that quickly reshaped to
show no evidence I'd ever pierced the surface.

"Come on, we gotta hurry. People around here
talk, they see ya on the street, and they'll report
you."

"How would they know I don't belong here?"

"They just do. You just sort of get a sense of
it once you're here long enough. Now stay close and
stop straying."

She marched me down the sidewalk in those
'Come Fuck Me' heels, ignoring the cat calls from
what looked like homeless men sitting on the sides
of buildings we passed. I heard a mutter, "Got a
soul? I'll pay good, I swear it. I'm good fo it man."

"Soul?" Dee's hand wrapped around the front of my shirt and tugged me after her. "Soul? Why's he want my soul?"

"Not yours in particular." She said, sounding a bit irritated. "Souls here are like a drug. Junkies steal them, and shoot them up. The high is similar to heroin mixed with acid. It's pretty fucking intense."

"But how-"

"Don't' bother. You wouldn't understand, even if I could think of a way to explain it to you in a simple enough way. There's where we need to be."

She pointed up ahead, where China Theatre was spelled in light bulbs across an old Victorian structure. "A theatre?" I asked.

"Just follow. You ask too many questions."

"Everyone around here is some sort of monster, or disfigured, why do you seem normal?"

She laughed hard, "I'm not."

"Then what is wrong with you?"

"Well, there isn't really anything wrong with anyone here. Things are just different here. We are all different. You're different too."

"How? I think I'm pretty normal compared to most of the people of seen around here."

"That's the first sign something isn't right."

"What is?"

"The fact you think you're normal. Think about all the shit you've gone through since you got to where you are now. Really think you're just fucking normal?"

"Well, more so than what I've seen."

She wheeled around, her expression contorted, "I'm a werewolf. That's my thing, I'll turn in another couple hours like I do every night. But instead of being at home in my room, locked up where I'm safe, I'm out here helping you." She turned and continued on towards the theatre. "You aren't normal. You are dead with a heartbeat."

"I haven't died though."

"Something in you did, or you'd give a shit about someone other than yourself."

"I do. Helen and Alice are my world."

"No, they're your distraction from the world. When you see the world, you are so disconnected, you might as well be a star in the sky watching what happens on the ground. You belong here, with or without a beating heart." She pushed open the door. A crowd stood in line for popcorn, beer, and pizza. So much like the real world.

We brush by, shoving and swimming through, over to an open door on the right. We enter, the pathway lit by small, dim lights along the lavishly carpeted floor. As we step away from the wall, seats come into view. The theatre is empty, everyone getting snacks I suppose. She marches me right up to the screen, "You will be back, and it will be soon. When it happens, come see me, I'll help again. I'm just that pathetic I guess. But let me tell you this, you will have a hard time getting back if you don't end this preoccupation with self-loathing. You are as miserable as you've made yourself. Remember that."

Ignoring her message, "So what do I do now?"

She huffed, "Step through the screen, asshole."

"What?"

"Oh, fuck, I'm not gonna hold your hand the whole way." She extended her arm, pushing it through the screen. Instead of pressing against the canvas, her hand plunged into whatever laid beyond, "Just walk through it." She pulled her hand back.

I step up to the screen, and press my hands against, I feel coldness spread along my skin. I look once more at Dee, "I know you're mad at me, but thanks for your help." Then I take a breath and dive into the screen.

No Longer Your Concern

Chapter Eleven

"Ezra! Ezra, wake up!" I open my eyes to find Efren looking down at me. He has a wild and panicked look in his eyes, and is covered in blood. His shirt soaked, pants ripped, his eyes looking too bright in the darkness around them. "Come on, we gotta get the hell out of hear." The grinding rumble of hundreds of voices groaning at once tears through the air. I take the hand he offers, and he pulls me to my feet. He is already starting to run, tugging at my shirt, "Run, now!" I did.

It's dark, I have no idea how he can possibly see where we are going. I can barely make out the trees, and long shadows hanging off of the branches. We ran another fifty yards when I finally realize the shadows are bodies hanging from nooses tied to the branches. They wave and rock, trying to get their hands on us, moaning painfully, struggling to get free from the ropes holding them up.

"Where are we?!"

"No idea, but I'm pretty sure we shouldn't be here."

"Where's Helen and Alice?"

"Don't know. Alice took off on us. We were chasing after her when we heard a scream. Jump!" I did, glad he'd warned me in time to clear a narrow canal, filled to the brim with rushing water. "She screamed, that's when these guys started going ape shit. We were running towards the sound when I spotted you. I stopped, told Helen to keep going. She was heading this way when she left me."

The ground crunches loudly beneath my feet. Whatever is beneath my feet definitely isn't the usual dirt and leaves. My back and neck burned. I caught a glimpse of my hands and find that they are covered in blood, "What the hell happened to me? What happened to you?"

"The blood?" He glances back without slowing his stride, "The ground is covered in broken glass. I tripped earlier. I'm guessing when you arrived you landed on it as well."

"I don't remember passing out. I just stepped through the screen."

"There's a lot I don't remember. Something is going on."

"What do you mean?" A scream from our right, we shift directions. I slip, sliding on my side and thigh across the glass. It feels like fire running over my skin before I can manage to push myself back up and continue running.

"Well, for starters, do you remember the flight to Alaska? Like, at all? Cause I don't."

I thought about it, but I don't recollect it at all. I didn't remember boarding the plane, being on the plane at all, or getting to the airport. After the last night at Efren's, I just remember seeing Annie and already being at the cabin. I didn't even remember picking up Alice from Norman. "I don't."

"What about the first few days after arriving at the cabin? I remember getting there, walking in, then nothing til the night Vincent arrived."

Again, I had no recollection of the time in between. Yet I hadn't noticed it at the time.

"Something ain't right, man. Something has been fucking with us since Helen disappeared."

"Like what though?"

"No fucking clue. There, a light?" He points towards a spot two hundred yards in front of us. It looks like someone swinging a torch left and right. We approach quietly and I can now make out Helen swinging the torch. Some of the bodies had gotten loose and were closing in on Helen and Alice.

"Hey! Hey, you fucking bastards!" The things from the tree's turned to look at me, "Get them out of here, Efren."

"What are you going to do?"

I don't answer. I divert to my right, with the things in tow, chasing me down with speed that I hadn't expected them to have. Weaving through the orchard in near darkness, I keep a wary eye on the even darker shadows of trees. A pair of boots smash into my face. My head flings back, my feet swing into the air. I crash to the ground, scrambling to my feet, shards of glass slicing into the skin of my hands. I can hear the footsteps of my pursuers pounding nearer.

Taking two more steps, I tumble headlong into the canal. As the current sweeps me down, the memory of Efren and I at the river so long ago comes to me.

My head slams into the ditch bank, spinning my body wildly. I fight my way to the surface, desperate to avoid getting tangled in debris I imagine waiting underneath. My fingers scrabble at the crumbling embankment but I am moving too fast to catch hold.

Ahead in the darkness, I hear grunts over the roaring water. In the distance I can make out a few of the inhuman creatures kneeling at the water's edge, waiting and watching. Trying to get centered in the current, I push myself left, then right, hoping to regain a measure of control and stay centered. I reach out to push again, but something catches my hand. The grip is tight, then sharp pain as teeth sink into the meat of my palm. My head submerged as I feel the agony of another bite on the same hand. I screamed, but it was just a loud gurgle. I don't know if they let go, or the current ripped me away, but I am released, free and back on my watery journey.

Soon the trees are gone, and moonlight begins shining around me. The roar of water surrounds the air around me. I am heading for a cliff, a waterfall. The canal widens, so I start swimming towards the bank, but get nowhere within my struggle. I give up.

So this is how it happens? I don't feel that guilt she mentioned. I see a vast body of water before me. As I roll with the water off the edge, I spin through the air like an Olympic gymnast. "This is gonna fucking hurt." I mutter to myself. After the first few spins, I've lost all sense of orientation. Up, down, side to side, they all mean nothing as the rocky base of the waterfall spins in and out of my view, growing ever nearer. Just then, flapping wings approach, and then something has me in its arms, carrying me off towards land.

Gently releasing me to the ground, the angel lands near me.

"Why are you here?" She asks angrily.

"You told me to come."

"I did no such thing."

"You showed up at my apartment and told me I had to get here with Alice. It was the only way to get Helen back."

"I did not. Helen belongs here."

"No she doesn't. She vanished just like my parents."

The angel tilts her head, a look of confusion on her face, "Is that so?"

"Yes."

"You need to leave. Helen will have to stay. And the girl, well the girl is no longer your concern. But you have to leave." Her eyes drop towards my hand, "And you need to wrap that. If you die here, you die in your world too."

Looking down at my hand, the moonlight reveals the gruesome sight. My fingers are mangled, half missing, my palm torn to shreds, blood streaming.

"Follow that trail." She points at a dirt path that wound through a hillside covered in trees. "Once there, you'll find someone waiting to help you."

"I won't leave without Helen, Alice, and Efren."

She closes her eyes, "Efren is already dead. The others cannot leave. Take this opportunity, you will not receive another one." Then she takes back to the sky, leaving me staring up at her.

When she is out of my sight, I turn towards the path, and begin walking.

The Worst Day of My Life

Chapter Twelve

I take my time walking up the hillside. The trees smell like Spruce, but look nothing like it. Instead they appear dead and withered, not a single leaf hangs from a scraggly branch. The trail is coming to an end, light shines in the distance, my destination awaited. But what was waiting there, or better yet, who?

My breath leaves me when I reach the top of the hill. I find myself in a cul-de-sac, and on the sidewalk, stands Efren. I ran to him, giving him a hug, "The angel told me you were dead."

"I am." He says.

I step back, releasing him from my embrace, "But..."

"It's the land of the dead, man." He said with a laugh, "I didn't have far to go. It's all good though, no worries, I'm content. Don't beat yourself up over it, wasn't your fault."

"Yeah, it is! How do you not see that? If it weren't for me, we would have never come here."

"Yeah we would have." he said with a smile, "Believe me, you'll understand soon enough. You didn't have a choice, none of us did."

"What do you mean? Of course we had a choice."

"No, we didn't. Now go. There is still much you have to see. I'm sorry, it won't be pleasant, and I won't be there to help you through. But we'll see each other again, sooner than either of us would like. Good luck, my friend." Then he shoves me off the sidewalk. The moment my feet touch the asphalt, the ground gives way.

Plunging feet first into a body of water, I kick my feet to try and reach the surface, but every kick just carries me deeper. I give up and let the water pull me wherever it wants me to be.

Then, in an instant, I find myself sitting on the balcony of my apartment, on my plastic bench. A cigarette in hand, the sun beating down on me hot and heavy. I squint, looking into the glare of the aluminum top of a carport.

I drop the cigarette, stepping on it as I stand from the bench. Walking into the apartment, it looks as it had before the fire. Walking passed the kitchen, I see smoke drifting from the living room. Upon entering, I find Annie sitting on the couch smoking a cigarette, with my bottle of Jack sitting on the coffee table. When she looks up at me though, I realize it isn't Annie. It resembles her, but subtle features were different. The nose is more narrow, her eyes not as bright, her hair slightly darker.

"Sit down, Ezra." I'm stunned, rendered speechless. Like a zombie I make my way to sit beside her. "Don't recognize me?"

"Alice? How..." Before my eyes she transformed back to the five-year-old girl I remembered. Then back to the woman who stood before me.

"That whole time, you envisioned a little girl, and you are so lost in your own trips that it didn't dawn on you how much time had passed since we last saw each other. You pathetic bastard." Had it been that long? It had only been three years. I was sure of it. She looked what, sixteen, maybe seventeen? "Sixteen prick. Eight years. Not three. Eight. You and your fucked up buddies were gone a little longer than it felt, weren't you?" No way. We were gone only for a few hours, or so it felt.

I look her over, the remnants of the little girl had been covered with crimson lipstick, heavy mascara and eyeliner. A little goth, just like her mother had been when we'd first met.

"Time moves differently in the other realms." She is almost laughing before she came to a sudden stop, "You think I wouldn't find out the truth? About who my parents are?"

"It wasn't a secret Helen planned on keeping. When you were old enough, she was supposed to tell you."

"Well she didn't. But I did figure it out. No thanks to you."

"How'd you figure it out?" She had a crassness, bitterness, similar to my own. I hadn't always had it, not until after Annie died. Had I caused this? She was such a happy little girl. Always smiling and laughing, jumping around, always so playful and carefree.

"Yeah, you are the one that fucked me up. Don't question it at all." I am taken off guard. "I got this talent, from you actually. That's why you could always control the dreamer drugs so well, your brain is wired differently. So is mine. I learned how to use it without the drugs though. I can make people see and do what I want them to. Whether they know it or not."

"So all of what I just went through, it wasn't real?"

"Oh, it was real. I met Vincent a long time ago. We met in first grade. We were the only ones we'd trust our secrets too. My story isn't why I'm here though."

"So what is it you want?"

"I put the pieces together when I looked you up online and noticed the features that matched. Then I found a picture of you and Annie together, and everything lined up. There isn't anything about her that I can find online though. Helen told me a little bit here and there about my 'Aunt Annie'. But not enough. I want you to tell me about her."

"I can do that. We didn't have to go through all of this to do that."

"Yeah we did. Believe me, there's a lot more to this. Now start."

"Well, your mother, she was... she was beautiful. Most beautiful woman I'd ever seen. She was kind of a smartass, but never mean. She had this way of reading a person, and picking up on their emotions. She'd tell you exactly what was bothering you before you could speak a word."

I reach down and grab the bottle from the table, take a drink, put the bottle back, then light a cigarette. "She loved you like crazy. Every chance she got she'd be holding you or playing with you. She absolutely adored you."

"How'd she die?"

"That was the worst day of my life. It doesn't really matter. What matters is that she loved you. She was a wonderful person, the best I'd ever met."

"They say you went crazy after you wrote the book about her."

"I did. I totally lost it. Helen and Efren had to follow me to hell to bring me back. If it wasn't for them, I wouldn't be here now."

"Tell me. The day she died. Tell me everything you remember. That day and after. Tell me how you suffered." She smirks. I look into those eyes, and they are so cold. So unlike her mothers. How had I caused so much damage and not realized it? How had I not seen her or gotten to know this person sitting before me? I had been selfish I guess. Lost in my own recklessness and lack of fucks to give about anything else in my life.

"Tell me, now." It was an order. So I begin...

Our New Bed

Chapter Thirteen

The day paints itself perfectly in my mind, like it did every time it spilled across my thoughts.

"Since I'd known your mother, she'd always had these fits of depression. And after you were born, they seemed to vanish. When you turned five though, they resurfaced. I'm not sure why. I think about it all the time. If something happened that triggered it, and nothing ever comes to mind. But there they were, with a vengeance. Making up for lost time I suppose. It was just so much worse than it had been before. The little fits of the past seemed so small compared to what it had become." I smother my cigarette, then light another. Take another drink from the Jack, then sigh. I really didn't want to do this right now, but I guess there never would be a right time.

"The cabin in Alaska, it was our dream home. That night we'd gotten the word that our bid had been accepted. We got it. We were so excited." I dragged from the cigarette, remembering Annie's reaction when we got the call. Her eyes lighting up, jumping around, rambling on in a speedy jumble of words I could barely understand as she began listing things we'd need.

"That night, we sat on the bed surfing the web. The most important thing to us was a bed. Sounds stupid, I know. But to us, it was a big fucking deal. Although my first novel had done so well, the money didn't last that long. I was picking up small jobs for sketches and stuff, but nothing that made us enough to keep afloat. Your mom worked over at Gallery 55, downtown. We barely cut even on bills. Everything we had was second hand. We'd never had anything new. Then we got word they were making the movie, I signed the paperwork, and boom, the first big check came. Life was good again.

The cabin was cheap. As you've seen, it's pretty bare. But the bed, it had to be perfect.

"We decided to go to some of the furniture stores the next day, find one we liked, then find it online up in Alaska, having it delivered when we made our way there."

I take another drink from the bottle before carrying on, "That night she was so giddy. She wanted to wake you up and tell you all about it. I told her no, we'd tell you about it in the morning. Show you some of the pics we had on the laptop. She was fidgeting all night, her feet kicking like you would in our bed when you were just a baby." I stare down at my lap, letting the tears that had welled in my eyes start to fall.

"When I woke the next morning, she was still asleep. I called Helen, she would watch you while we were out looking at beds. I knew you would get bored at the store, then start going all crazy. I woke up your mom, told her I was going to drop you off. I told her to get dressed and we'd go grab some breakfast first. I kissed her. She kissed me hard back, like she had when we'd first started seeing each other. We didn't kiss like that so often anymore. But that morning, it was different. I thought it was a good thing. Little did I know it was her saying goodbye, in a way."

I stand, considered pacing the living room, a habit of mine when talking or thinking, but sit back down instead.

"I dropped you off, and came right back. Maybe all of ten minutes had passed. When I walked in, I heard her sobs. I shut the door and went to the bathroom where the sobs came from. I..." I had to stop for a moment. A knot in my throat had formed, my mouth suddenly very dry. I drink from the bottle, smothering the butt of my smoke. I take a deep breath, calming myself as much as possible. "She sat cross-legged on the floor. Blood was all around her. The left inner forearm was sliced open wide, the fingers of her right hand digging in, tearing at the veins and muscle. She just kept saying, 'I can't get it out of me.' Over and over. I asked what, I asked again, she wouldn't reply. I fought to get her arms separated, then pulled the towel from the rack by the shower, wrapping it tight. I dialed 911 on my cell as I had her pinned down, putting pressure on her arm. I held her as she started slipping away, pleading with her to just hang on a little longer. Then, right before she closed her eyes she said, 'I can't get the dark out.' She closed her eyes, and they never opened again. The medics came and did what they could. But she'd lost too much blood already. By the time they got to the hospital, she was gone."

I stop, light another cigarette, take a drink, look at Alice, and see no emotion in her face. "In two weeks, I did two things. Helen watched you so I could grieve, you didn't seem to even notice your mother was gone. You had so much fun with Helen. Anyways, two things happened. I went shopping for our new bed. I looked everywhere before deciding on the one I'm sure your mother would have wanted. I ordered it, and had it delivered to the cabin. Then I wrote the book. In between was the funeral. To be honest though, I was so fucked up, I can't remember anything about it other than sitting at her grave after everyone left, crying until it felt like my brain was going to seep from my tear ducts. That night, I tried to shoot myself. I was too high though, my hand wavered, the bullet grazed the back of my head, hit a beam in the wall of the apartment, ricocheted back and hit my chest. It had already lost most of its momentum by that point. It didn't have the juice left to punch through.

"I laid there bleeding, and that was when she appeared to me. The angel sat beside me, running her fingers through my hair. She whispered in my ear, telling me I had more to do, that I had to be strong. That I had to be strong for you. She said you were important. I heard banging on my door, then the angel was gone. My door flung open, the door frame shattering as two cops ran in. Then I remember nothing until I woke up in the hospital. I ended up getting a thirty-day hold, then was released. As soon as I was free, I flew straight to the cabin, didn't tell a soul. Just left."

Some Sins Require Sacrifice

Chapter Fourteen

"Well now, isn't that a nice little story. Now we move on." She waves her hand and we are no longer in my apartment. I find us at the foot of the pool out back of Efren's. "I must apologize. Things progressed more slowly than I had originally intended. Honestly, I kind of started having a little too much fun watching you guys run around scared out of your minds." She giggles in such a girlish manner that I almost started thinking maybe she isn't bat shit crazy after all. It is short lived though, a moment later the coldness is back, "You want to see how you killed all your friends?"

"I didn't kill anyone."

"Oh yeah you did. Well, I guess in a way, you were more of a bystander than anything. I did it, but I did it as you. All those blank spots, the strange mockingbird experience, my doing. All of it while I inhabited your mind, forcing your conscious to sit in a chair in the darkest corner of your head."

"What did you do?!" She begins walking into the house, I follow closely behind. As we step upon the cracked tile of the room where we'd played beer-pong just a week before, I notice bloody footprints smeared across the floor. But the biggest shock is Zoe. She stands before us smiling wildly, excited.

"You're alive?" She gives me a snide glance, then beams back at Alice.

"She's here for me." Alice walks up and kisses Zoe hard, Zoe's hands grip onto Alice's ass, pulling her tightly against herself. Alice breaks away, "Zoe's got this talent. She can die, and when her soul leaves her body, she can recreate it with the particles floating around nearby. It's really quite profound. See, as she stands here," Alice steps behind Zoe, "solid as we are," Alice puts her hands on Zoe's breasts, giving them a squeeze, "her body is also laying bloated and bludgeoned on your bed." They both start laughing manically.

I bolt towards the bedroom, the stink of rot shoving itself into my nostrils as I reach the hall. Upon opening the bedroom door, thick and heavy air jumps down my throat, causing me to vomit instantly all over the floor. The scene is awful. Laying on her stomach, Zoe's body is gray and swollen, looking slimy, almost liquid. Blood has caked along the walls, the bed, and over her body, her head split wide open.

Alice approaches the corpse, leaning over and kissing Zoe's lips. When she pulls away, strands of what was once flesh stick and stretch against her own lips, "Still so fucking gorgeous. Isn't she?" Alice wipes away the left over slime across her lips from Zoe's own as an afterthought.

Zoe moves beside Alice, examining her body, "Wish you'd have given me a little warning. Didn't know you were going to be so rough."

"Ha, I gave it to you easy compared to Robin."

"No. I don't get it, why would you do this, Alice? I get I wasn't there for you, but come on, it's not worth all this."

"It is though. The lies you guys made me live were one thing, the abandonment another, but even that isn't the part that really gets me. If you'd just kept your shit together, and spent some time with me, we could have brought mom back."

I am torn, between the gut-wrenching possibility that this is true, or if it is just Alice fucking with me further. If it was true, oh god, it can't be true. It just can't be. "What are you talking about, she was dead, there's no bringing her back."

"Zoe could have brought her back. It's part of her gift. But because you let so much time pass, it's too late for her, she's in another place."

"But I saw her, when we were in Alaska."

"She can come when she wishes to. But she can't come back to being now. Once you pass from the land of the dead, you lose the power to control the environment in our world. But before passing to the next realm, you can still regain your life. But only a few, like Zoe, know how to do it. Everything could have been different. Instead you just laid there in pity and sorrow for yourself. We missed our window, setting our path in stone. And now here we are, without her, wasted years in between. It's your fault we are like this, it's your fault we're so fucked up!" she screams at me.

"On with it, show him already." Zoe barks impatiently. She turns to Alice, shoving her hand down the crotch of her cutoff shorts, "I want to see it again." Alice leans her head back, eyes rolling back while she moans. Beneath the shorts I can see Zoe's hand jerking up and down, "Come on, babe. Let's watch it again."

"Okay, okay." Alice lunges out, her hand phasing right into my head, then it all goes black.

I'm opening my eyes to a blur. Light is dim in the room; I'm trying to focus. I begin to move, but I have no control over the motion. Looking over at Zoe's naked body beside me, I slowly slip out of the bed. Naked and not bothering to dress, I quietly open the bedroom door and peer into the hall. Efren and Robin are still sleeping. In a hurry, I'm moving down the hall, through the kitchen, into the garage. Examining the tables and tool boxes, I'm looking for something, although I have no idea what.

My eyes land upon a lump hammer. I grab it, and a screwdriver resting on top of the tool box, then leave the garage. Walking back into the kitchen, I turn left towards the stereo near the sliding door that leads to the pool. I put a cd in, push play. As I walk away, "For Love Not Lisa" starts to blare loudly through the house.

On my way back to the room, I peer in on Efren and Robin, they haven't been awakened by the music yet. Setting the hammer and screwdriver down on the bed, I pull the sheet away from Zoe. Looking over her naked body, I lean over and roll her slowly onto her stomach. I straddle her, and she begins to stir. Quickly, I grab the hammer, and wait for her to wake completely. Her eyes slowly flutter open. "What are you doing, Ezra?"

"Not Ezra." I say.

"Alice?" She then spots the hammer in my hand, held in the air. "Damnitt. Why a fucking hammer?" Then I bring the hammer down into her skull. She begins jerking around beneath me after the impact. I smack her ass and begin laughing hysterically. I'm bouncing around on her like I'm at a fucking rodeo. I swing the hammer again, then her body slows, writhing a little, but slowly losing its life. I feel warmth under my ass, looking down I see that she's pissing all over the bed and me as her body continues to stay tense and struggle with what little force is left. For some reason, I drill the hammer into her skull once more, this time her skull cracks wide, sending blood and chunks of bone and brain matter across the walls, the bed, and myself. Stepping off of her, I look at her body, and slam the hammer against her spine, hearing a loud *snap*at the impact. When I pull the hammer back, I see the break between the vertebrae beneath her skin. I bring the hammer down again, and again, against the spine, her ribs, neck. Each impact meeting Zoe's body with a smack like a ribeye being slapped onto a butchers table. When I finally stop, bone protrudes from the skin, blood is splattered over her, flecks on the ceiling, over my own body, painted across my forearm near the hammer, and I want to puke. Instead, I feel giddy, I feel pleased with myself. Not me though, no, it's Alice. My hands trace over the curves of Zoe's body, leaving trails through the blood. I cup her ass, giving it a squeeze, finding I'm getting a hard on through this process, although it's technically Alice's hard on, I guess.

I pick up the screw driver and leave the room. Crossing the hall, I quietly open Efren's bedroom door. Zoe is standing by the edge of the bed where Robin lays sprawled out deep in sleep. Efren is sleeping in the fetal position on the floor.

With her hands she motions towards Efren and points at me. I'm walking up to where he lies, then kneeling down. Zoe hops onto the bed and pins herself against Robin who wakes with a scream. As she does so, I shove the screwdriver into the temple of Efren's head. His eyes and mouth open wide, but no sound comes out. His body tightens, but doesn't move. Pulling the screwdriver out, I plow it into his throat, then do it again. He never fights back, just bleeds and twitches, his eyes locked onto the wall in front of him.

I watch him intently, Alice had every intention of me seeing this the whole time, looking down into his eyes as they died. My friend, the one constant in my life aside from Helen. Wanting so much to do something for him, to save him. *Where is the angel now?*

Robin screams and strains to fight off Zoe who is relentless in her restraint. Peeling my focus away from Efren, I mount the bed. Taking hold of Robin's arms, Zoe moves and straddles her legs. She leans over and pulls the screwdriver from Efren's neck.

"Do what you gotta do." I say before she starts plunging the screwdriver into Robin's stomach. She does so twice more, then drops the screwdriver onto the floor. Zoe buries her fingers into the holes she made with the screwdriver. She fits in three fingers, then pulls. I see the muscle in her forearm flex and struggle before the flesh gives way and tears from Robin. With an opening, before I can see much of what lies beneath, Zoe boroughs her head in and begins eating. Robin screams, she tries to fight, her voice growing hoarse. I swear her throat must be bleeding by the time she finally begins to get faint. Her body still flexed, tight, wanting to fight, but running out of strength. She's tired, dizzy, I can tell by the way her eyes are bouncing around slowly, unable to keep focus on anything around her. The muscles begin to loosen, her body losing the rigidity from the initial state. She is going soft, she is dying, and her eyes seem more desperate as the seconds tick by. Mouth still agape, air escaping, but sound has been lost to her. I stand watching as Zoe continues to eat for almost another hour. Watching turns me (or the Alice in me) on even more than before. Grabbing my hard on, I plunge it between Robin's legs. I thrust hard, she barely registers it seems. Zoe pulls her head away from her feast and kisses me. She raises herself up, placing her nipple into my mouth as I begin to suckle on it. I grab her ass and pull her against me as I continue fucking Robin. Moving my hand to her crotch, I slip my fingers in, feeling the moisture flooding inside of her. She's just as turned on as Alice by all of this.

Then the voice starts. It's Alice in my head. "This is your life! This is what you brought upon yourself and everyone you loved! We could have saved her. You killed her, abandoned me, and now everyone you care about is dead."

"What about Helen?" I think. Then everything changes again.

I'm no longer at Efren's. I am now at Norman and Helen's house, standing in the living room. Norman lies on the couch sleeping, Zoe standing beside him, then points at a prescription bottle in her other hand. Ambien, the label says. We walk away, up the stairs, then leave the hallway at the top. We enter the master bedroom, where Helen is folding clothes. I walk up behind her, then slam the lump hammer into the back of her head. She drops, clinging to the spot of impact, dazed and confused. Her free hand reaches for the frame of the bed, but the blood that comes away with her hand from her head causes her grip to slip, she falls back to the carpet.

Zoe is standing over her, squirting lighter fluid over her clothing.

"Open your mouth!" I say. "The hole that spreads your lies must be cleaned!" I grip onto her jaw and pull her mouth open as Zoe starts spraying the lighter fluid inside. Helen gags, tries to spit, but I cover her mouth. She's crying, trying to speak to me, to reason presumably. But I don't give her a chance. Zoe lights a match, I open Helen's mouth again, and Zoe drops the match. We jump away from Helen as flames dance in her mouth. She stands, screaming in a weird pitch. The flames are beginning to spread down her clothes, but the flesh around her mouth is where my eyes are focused. The skin blistering and charring. Her eyelashes catch, then her eyebrows. She's trying to run out of the room. I don't think she knew where she was going, she wasn't thinking straight, understandably. She hit the wall beside her closet, stumbled, then ran into the closet door. I swing the hammer, it crashes into her face, and she drops. Burning alive and not realizing it, better than sitting and feeling it, I think.

Then we're gone again.

I know where I am, and I'm back in control. My writing room, looking down at sketches of the angel.

"What do you feel?" Alice asks. Her tone calmer, almost sympathetic.

"Why does it matter?"

"I'm curious."

I think for a moment before answering. Remembering it all over again, everything that had happened, that I'd seen. I'd created this monster. Unknowingly, but I'd still done it. Helen, Efren, dead and gone. Maybe I could have brought Annie back, was that what she'd wanted? The burden of my presence in their lives had stolen their futures, their existence. I was a plague, a disease, and they were my victims. "Guilt. Shame. Disgust. At a loss really."

"Then it's time."

"Time for what?"

"Time for you to die." She looks sad. "Believe it or not, there is a love I have for you. You are my father after all." She stands, lights a cigarette and begins walking out of the room before turning back towards me, "But some sins require sacrifice. You are mine. Remember that. This isn't your pain or retribution. This is me paying for your sins." I see tears begin to trail down her face, "Come. We have somewhere to be." Then she exits the room.

Something More

Chapter Fifteen

As I walk out of the room, I find myself entering the cabin. Alice stands in front of me, Zoe is gone. Everything is coated in dust, smelling musky. The air tastes heavy with moisture as I inhale. It didn't look like it had when we'd been here before. "It's been eight years; it's collected a bit."

"If I was gone so long, how'd the apartment still look fine? And Efren's house? How are they still even ours?"

"Efren's isn't. It's been abandoned since they found the bodies. I kept your place. Zoe and I have been living there since Helen and Norman died."

"Norman's dead?"

"Yeah, turns out I miscalculated the amount of pills I gave him. Oops." But she has lost the humor to her malice. Her shell was beginning to crack.

"Come." She leads me up the stairs, to the bedroom. The bed is still covered in plastic, the receipt sitting on top, "You never even unwrapped it."

"But we slept on it."

"You were never here. You guys never left Efren's."

"But..."

"Things aren't as they seem. Here, I am sixteen. In actuality, I'm 28 now. You're in a version of the world that exist only to me. Think of it as a cell, larger than one you'd find in a prison, but one that does have boundaries. To be honest, the things I'm capable of, you couldn't even fathom, old man. In my version of reality, you died of an overdose. The world is about to end. There are creatures that roam the streets that you couldn't imagine, a war that has been waged that no one will truly win. But as I am there, I am here."

"I won't lie, I don't really get it all." I
replied, amazed at the lack of conviction in my
voice. Sounding tired, no rage, or will to fight left
at all.

"I wouldn't expect you to." She sits on the
bed, "I don't understand why I remember nothing
before living with Helen. I wish I did. I wish I
remembered her more. Little glimpses, moments,
sometimes I dream of her voice. But I'm not sure if
it is actually her voice, or just something my mind
made up." She stands back up and walks into the
room beside the bedroom. Along the walls were
pictures of Annie I'd taped up when I'd come here
right after her death.

"She looks so happy in all of these. I wish I
could have each of these moments in my mind. To see
it happening, to hear her, to feel her. I know I
can't, I can't even travel to that part of my mind.
It's like I put a lock on it and lost the key. What
I wouldn't give though. Maybe I'd be different. We'd
both be different, I suppose. I've done terrible
things. Awful things. Things I never thought I'd be

capable of." She turns and puts her finger to my forehead.

I'm looking down a broken street. The asphalt riddled with cracks, fires burn around me, bodies lay bloody and rotting. In the distance I hear screams, and the sound of buildings crumbling. "You wouldn't believe what happens in the future. There's so many that are like me. Like you. Do you recognize this place?"

"No."

"Maybe this will help." The scene morphs. We're sitting on a bench, looking at a river of fire. I turn, see demolished buildings behind me, the bridge to the right is broken, half sunken into the river. Chunks of concrete still breach the surface.

"Remember it now?"

"The river where her and I met?"

"Yup. Not quite the same as you remember though."

"What happened? What is going on here?"

"Nothing that you can make a difference towards." She snapped her fingers, and everything looked as it had so long ago. "This is two years ago."

"How do you even know about this place?"

"I know your thoughts. One of my many skills."

We're back at the cabin. "What happens now?"

"Whatever is meant to happen." She begins walking out of the cabin, I chase after her.

"Wait. I thought I was going to die?"

She stops, we face each other on the porch, the wind blowing her hair, her eyes squint a little. Then I see it, I see her mother in her, and it makes my heart ache. I smile. She reads my thought; I can tell by the way her face contorts slightly. She regains her composure, looks down at the warped planks under our feet, before she quickly kisses my forehead. "You're already dead." She turns and walks away, while pointing to the left as she scurries up the driveway, then vanishes.

I look where she pointed. A large tree beside
the cabin. And from a thick branch, I hang from a
rope. I'm lifeless, the wind causing me to sway a
little, side to side. I can't stop looking, almost
waiting for something more to happen, but of
course, nothing does. I look around, and I'm alone.
I'm all alone.

Day turns to night, and I sit on the steps to
the porch, waiting for some sign of what I'm
supposed to do. "Cigarette?" I jump, a little
startled. Annie sits beside me, holding out a smoke,
I take it. "Figure I owe you one after all these
years."

"I fucked up. I fucked up, Annie."

"You did. But it's okay. We still have time to
fix this."

"We can fix this?!"

"Not the way you want to. But we can stop her
from doing more harm."

"What is she doing? In the future I mean."

"Exactly what I told you she would. She's bringing the end of the world. She's changing everything. Destroying everything."

"Do we go to heaven or hell?"

"No."

"What happens then?"

"We stop Alice."

"But we're dead."

"Doesn't mean we can't do anything. The future holds a very complicated war between many realms. She is trying to destroy ours. Then she'll try to destroy others. But she isn't as aware of everything as she thinks she is. Nothings final, and nothings laid in stone. Despite how things seem sometimes. Some events can't be undone. But there is plenty that has yet to be written."

"How do we fix it then?"

Annie sighed, looks down at her feet, and without looking at me, answered. "We have to kill our daughter."

Epilogue (Mister Devereux)

What Really Lays Ahead?

A slick pair of shoes scrape across the cobblestone sidewalk. A hurried walk that breezes by a group of Dwarves that play dice atop an overturned cardboard box. Five gnarled faces with opium pipes hanging off of swollen lips, while rough, knobby hands scratch faces and asses before rolling the two die. Their voices are hoarse and low. The passing figure doesn't seem to notice them.

Swiftly making his way around the corner, narrowly avoiding a lamp post, and continuing towards the bar. He's anxious, slightly angry. His teeth clenched, the muscles of his jaw jutting from the sides of his face. His eyes are slightly squinted, illuminated by a cigarette pressed between his lips, the cherry glowing brightly as he drags off of it. He pulls it away with a shaky hand, thin tendrils of smoke slipping from his nostrils.

He stops under the neon sign, looking down at the wet sidewalk, finishing his cigarette. Voices from inside are loud, but the buzz from the sign overhead seem to damper the echo. Flicking the filter out into the road, and watching as it sank into the nothingness below, he turned away, facing the windows of the bar. Dee roams the path through the tables, a tray in one hand, using her other to grab empty bottles and plates from the table tops.

Glancing over the faces inside, his eyes come to rest on the back of a woman's head. He pauses, grunting slightly in disgust. Finally composing himself, he marches into the establishment. Dee pauses in her motions when she spots him, a slight gasp escaping her. He shakes his head, so that she knows he didn't bring Ariel. Making a beeline towards the woman sitting upon the stool at the bar instead.

Bojangles is sitting next to her, mumbling something about nothing as usual. The man taps upon his shoulder. The skeleton turns his face towards the man, "Oh no no, not again. Bojangles been good good, I swear it monsieur!"

The man pulls his head to the side, signaling Bojangles to move. With no hesitation, the boney figure rises from the stool and exits the bar without a second glance.

The man slides onto the stool as Dee walks up, her face still full of questions. "Whiskey, straight. Fill the glass, please."

"Never." She says with a smile.

He lights a cigarette and waits for his drink.

"Bad night, huh? Seems to be going around." The woman says.

Dee slides the glass to the man, then walks from the bar, silently signaling the other patrons sitting around to am-scray.

He sips from the glass, "Yours is about to get a lot worse."

The woman's body stiffens at the sound of the voice. She doesn't look, just continues to stare at the bottle of beer in her hand.

"You and your little bitch just put a whole lot of things into motion. Things that were never supposed to happen."

"I think you have me confused with someone else."

"I don't make mistakes. Neither does Ariel." A noticeable flinch. "She is very upset."

"But you aren't?"

"I am much beyond that. You killed someone I was pretty fond of. Ezra and I had become very close during our time of working together. He had a chance at really getting his life together. It was already planned. But you and that bitch, you guys ... You have no idea what you've done. What you gave her the ability to do."

"Listen, man. She fucked me over too, okay?"

"But the others you killed aren't like you. They're fucking dead. They can't come back. Their lives are over. That's it for them."

"I didn't know it would go so far."

"You were there while it did. You could have stopped it. At any time."

"She was too powerful for me."

"You could have called for Ariel. You chose not to."

"So, where is she? Aren't you here to finish me off?"

"As much as I wish I was, I am not. At least not yet. She has a job for you. A way to redeem yourself, in a manner of speaking."

"And what is this job?"

"You're to go back to the world of the living. You are going to help bring Alice down."

"How? She's too strong? Why doesn't Ariel do it?"

"Because the things you've put into motion, have had an effect on the world that has altered the reality itself. Ariel cannot step onto the

realm any longer. Not until Alice's control has
been stripped away. She's locked all the portals
into that realm. However, by being a human, you
could still pass back through."

"Sounds like an interesting proposition. But
Alice won't let me get near her. She'd kill me again
in a heartbeat."

"You won't have to. But you will guide the
others that can stop her. We can't get to them, so
you will be our messenger. There is only one other
that can traverse the realms, she will tell you
when we need you back here."

"If she can do it, why do you need me?"

"She has another purpose. Agree to these
terms, and you'll get to continue living your
disgusting life. Decline, and Ariel will take care
of you. Permanently."

"It must really bother you that she has you
here asking me a favor? Kinda funny, really."

He grabbed Zoe by the throat, lifting her off
the stool, into the air, then slammed her onto the
counter. He pulled a knife from his pocket, flicking

the bladed open, then pierced it through her ear. A scream escapes her while she struggles, but to no success.

"Ghost or living, I have the power to inflict whatever pain I wish upon you. Don't forget it. If I come to kill you, it will be slow, every second will be filled with more pain than the last, and it would bring me nothing but pleasure. I'd really like nothing more." He pulled the knife away, closing it and putting it back in his pocket before letting go of her throat. "But the call to make is not my own. Bigger things lie ahead, bigger than my hate for you."

Zoe coughed, her throat in pain from the grip.

"Now, are you interested in the offer or not?"

"Fine." She said hoarsely.

"Great. Have a seat, let's go over the details." He smothered his cigarette, lit another and finished his drink. "Dee, be a doll and fill me back up, will ya', hon?"

"Of course. Always a pleasure, Mr. Devereux."

"Oh, please, we know each other too well for that, darlin'. Call me Chris."

End Act One

I would like to thank you all for taking a trip through the first Act of this journey. Without the readers, friends, and followers, none of this would be possible. All my promotion and marketing really is ninety percent word of mouth and you guys sharing and following me on social media.

I'd give you all a billion dollars and a lifetime of happy moments never ending, if I could. But, you know, I can't! So instead, I will give you my word to weave the best stories I possibly can. The next Act is quickly coming to a conclusion, and it's an even wilder ride than this. Here's a chapter to give you taste.

Sign up for my mailing list/newsletter over at TheAfterLifeShow.com and get advanced copies of chapters right in your email, along with news on upcoming events/books going on in the world of 4 A.M., and much more nonsense on top of that!

Adieu Dear Hearts.

Yours Truly,

4 A.M.

The Art of Self-Destruction

Act Two:

Of

What Lies

Ahead

The earth rolled a dirty tongue through the crowd. Bodies were tossed loosely into the sky, flipping, somersaulting, limbs swinging wildly, eyes and mouths still caught in a moment before the moment. A rumble bled onto the rest of us way too graciously. So loud it hurt.

A cloud grew and widened from the rear, then propelled itself through the rest like a fountain pouring through cupped, thin and withered hands. Flowing onto the rest of us, bathing us in its massive particulate.

We would have kept playing, but we lost power. Our instruments fell silent, microphones no longer picking up our breath, lights flickered on-off-on-off before never coming back on. Freezing like statues upon the stage, we could only watch as the ground continued to catapult the crowd into the air, ripping apart, before striking the stage.

I couldn't pinpoint the moment my feet left the stage. The memory of being airborne is the only clear depiction of the moment. Inhale-exhale-inhale-don't fucking panic. I could see the mic stand, but it was sideways. Maybe two seconds had passed when I realized that the mic stand had stopped moving, but I had not. Reminded me of the first time I got really shitfaced at a party back in high school.

TWIST-TWIST-TURN-FLIP-TWIST.

The view sped by so fast, I had no way of knowing my ass from my face when I finally collided against hearth. Nauseas and aching, I was glad to be relatively stationary, although it was short lived.

My fingers dug into the dirt, trying to grasp on, but the world kept shaking me. Maybe it was the adrenaline, I thought. But as my eyes locked back on the crowd, I watched the flames spit from the mouth of a hole that once was the stage I'd been on just a minute or two before.

A delay hung in the air like unrecognized tension before crashing against me like a Mack truck. I was in the air, looking down, I could see my shadow. Bodies laid limp across the land my shadow came to cross like a low flying plane passing overhead. Light from the latest impact forced shards of darkness in every direction rhythmically, like a strobe light, following a beat I couldn't hear.

The inside of my mouth was dry and grainy from dirt shoving its way in while I'd screamed. I hadn't noticed it then. But thinking back, I remember screaming while airborne. I remembered specifically because I'd been screaming, but couldn't hear myself doing so at the time, because of the explosions around us.

My face crashed down into the dirt. I tasted blood almost immediately. When my jaw broke, I saw bright lights, but I tried to ignore them. I had to get the fuck out of here. I pushed myself up, and I started running.

My intentions, honestly, were to ignore everything and everyone that came into my view. Fuck them, I wanted to live. I mean, is that so wrong? To want to survive? To come out of this in one piece as I watched pieces of others thrust into the air without their collective selves?

Yet, as I was almost out of the stadium, exit in view, I saw her. Pinned down, a man on top of her, fighting, but not strong enough. I looked around. Others prayed, cried, ran, raped, fought. But here she was in front of me, just wanting to survive, and this asshole just wanted to get his giddy-up on before all hell rained onto the breathing being's that were still being.

DO IT OR DON'T-DO IT OR DON'T- I done did it. I jump on him. Crashing into him, we roll, and I'm swinging. I get lucky, one swing passes through his blocking arms, connects with his cheek, and he goes limp. Working back to my feet, the girl still lays on the ground, stunned. I help her up, "GETUPGETUPGETUP!!!!!" The pain in my face is awful, and my words are slurred, sounding lazy and fat as the syllables attempt to reach her ears. I tug her to her feet. She's still stunned, looking around, stumbling while I pull her towards the exit.

There's a loud sound from overhead. A tearing of the world we knew, as the giant ball of fire finally rips into our personal bubble. I just want out of the stadium, I don't know where I'm going after that, but my chances seem a lot better away from all the towering walls of concrete that are quickly trapping us all in for a case of certain death.

A clown steps in front of me. No shit, a fucking clown. He's standing there, his hand out, signaling stop. As I approach, he retracts his hand, and reaches behind his back, then reveals a miniature boat. I stop, watching, I mean, how could I not?

Setting it onto the ground, he grips the front and back with both hands, then grinds it into the ground a bit. Using his hands, without speaking, he motions for me to back up. We move back, although the woman looks at me like I'm crazy. The clown begins dancing, hopping foot to foot, shaking his hips, then spinning his arming like a windmill.

There's a bright flash, and the boat has grown into a full size speed boat. With his arms swinging, the clown motions for me to get in. So I do, and so does she. He smacks the back of the boat, and the motor starts up like a champ. Spitting out dirt from the rotor, and then the son of a bitch takes off like a speedster.

With backsplash of dirt tossed into the air behind us, we're speeding off towards the exit. As I see our destination, the existence around it is crumbling. The stadium is falling to pieces. A fog has spread around from the destruction. Across the ground are bodies and blood sprayed and soaking into the scene. A screen ahead shows me salvation, but the screen is breaking, it goes black and white. I'm losing signal. I want to adjust, but cannot. It is time, this is it, I'm fucked, I'm done, it's over, but I put up a hell of a fight. Does it matter? I don't know. I feel like I'm in a battle, but is there some entity I'm against? I want to say I'm winning. I want someone to scream, "I'm beating you!" at.

As I cross the threshold of the stadium exit, the rear of the boat is kicked into the air as another little ball of fire hits. I'm almost to the ground when I see her plunging face first into the asphalt. Her blood splashes across my face, the ground around us, the seat of the boat.

I wanted to save her. I failed. Then I made contact, and everything went black.

But I didn't stop thinking. I thought, If I survive this, I'm sssssooooo getting a Little Caesar's Deep Dish afterwards.